THE RISE OF EDEN

ASIN: B08Q6DPC83

Book Cover By: Damoro Designs

Publisher: Wicked Storm Publishing, LLC

Chapter One

"Well, this has turned into a bloody mess now hasn't it?" Silas's smooth and alluring voice came from the castle window that he had sat perched in, soaking in the warm rays of sun like a purple-haired cat, lounging about his business.

I, on the other hand, was freaking the fuck out.

"Don't move." I pointed a finger at Asher like it was a weapon of mass destruction that he should be afraid of.

He stood in front of the doorway that he had stumbled out of, the expression on his face looking just as confused as I felt.

I usually had no idea what the hell was going on, but this went above and beyond my usual level of confusion. It was different.

It was the kind of confusion that made your brain ache when you thought about it. But also the type that haunted you until you figured it out.

There he was, Asher, standing in front of me, flesh and bones. I knew that much was true.

But I also knew that I had seen a live stream of him out in the world, destroying something, right before we left.

And time was frozen.

So which Asher was THE Asher?

The one that I despised more than life itself.

Or was this just another one of those parlor tricks that the universe thought was so funny to pull? An illusion. Something that wasn't real.

The initial shock had worn off of Asher, and now he just leaned up against the doorway with his arms crossed, nothing but a smug smirk on his face.

He was trying to play it smooth, but I could tell by the look in his eyes, he was feeling lost too. He just didn't want to admit it.

"Is she always this aggressive?" He said with a smooth voice.

"To be honest, I'm not quite sure. We've only known each other for a few hours, but I'd suppose so. Isn't it enchanting?" Silas winked in my direction, and butterflies rose in my stomach.

"That's one word for it." Asher mumbled before he looked me up and down. I didn't know if it was to size me up or check me out.

Both maybe?

Outside, the sound of birds floated in from the window. It was weird, finally hearing them after the long silence that we'd endured.

The kingdom was coming alive again, and I had no idea what that meant if I was honest. Not a clue what the plan was.

And if I was being honest, having Asher in front of me made me uneasy.

How the hell was I supposed to save the world when the dick who put it in danger in the first place was standing there staring at me like a wild animal that could attack at any moment.

I opened my mouth to say something when Apollo burst through the doorway.

"Guys, whatever you did, it worked. Everyone woke-" His words were cut off when his gaze landed on Asher. "What the fuck?"

In the blink of an eye, he had a long strand of water pulled from his pouch, and it was sent sailing through the air. His face dropped into an angry scowl as he did.

It took Asher by surprise, but it didn't surprise me even a little.

I threw my hand out and sent a stream of fire through the air, evaporating the water before it had a chance to get to Asher.

Everyone in the room's eyes darted to me, all for different reasons probably. Apollo looked at me angrier than he ever had, which I thought must have broken some sort of world record. Silas just looked turned on, a glint of allure in his eyes at me flexing my power. But the change in Asher's face had to be the biggest, his jaw hung open, and he looked like he'd just seen a ghost.

A very impressive ghost, and for a second, I felt a wave of satisfaction that I was the one who put the look there in the first place, but I caught myself.

There's nothing good about impressing him. I reminded myself. *He's a fucking monster.*

I didn't really know why I did it anyway. It was Asher. I hated his guts- or I should have.

He stole my best friend, exposed the worst parts of her, railed her a few hundred times, and a billion other things, including almost turning me into a homicidal pyromaniac in charge of burning down half of my city.

And when I thought of those things, it was true. I did hate him. I hated his guts and every single fiber of his being.

But there was something when I looked at him that didn't make him feel like the same person. Sure, he was missing the long scar that ran through his eye, but it went further than that. It was about the vibe he threw off all the other times I had come into contact with him. He had an energy that surrounded him, one that made your skin crawl and your teeth hurt. It was like he was stuffed with so much rage at everyone in the world that it oozed off of him and created his own anger-filled atmosphere. Everyone felt it.

Hell, you could be halfway down the street and still feel it when Asher passed through.

But there, I didn't feel it. All the anger, and rage, and hostility that used to cling to the air whenever he was near was gone, and instead, I felt something softer around the edges. The hot, angry power was still there, but this time it left a different taste in my mouth.

Maybe that was why I did it. It was a reflex, more like protecting a stranger. I didn't feel like he was guilty of anything, not at that moment.

"How the hell did he get here? And what is so fucked up in your mind that you would defend him like that?" Apollo spit the words out in my direction, his anger seething even more than usual.

He took a step toward me, but I wasn't scared. I knew he wouldn't dare touch me.

He was a douchebag, but he wasn't on that level. There was more than just anger in his eyes. There was a level of pain that I hadn't seen before.

He was hurting, and I had no idea why.

But what happened next was something that I wouldn't have expected in a million years. I would have anticipated hell to freeze over before anything like it ever happened.

Asher finally moved away from the doorway and placed himself in between Apollo and me, like a human shield.

"Apollo, chill. Don't fucking talk to a woman like that. Have you lost your fucking mind?" His voice was a confused growl.

I thought I was confused before all of that shit happened, but I realized I didn't know what confusion was until those words had left his lips.

It was like I died and was sent to confused heaven.

"What?" Apollo and I both said at the same time.

The shock of it all was enough to knock Apollo out of his angry streak.

Before we could say anything else, Atlas helped Adler stumble through the door, still a little sore.

"Holy shit." I rushed to their side and threw my arms around both of them. "I'm so glad you're okay." I sighed.

But I didn't have their full attention, which was evident by the way that their jaws hung open.

"I don't have a single idea of what the fuck is going on." I whispered in both of their ears with my back turned to Asher.

"Adler, Atlas! I'm so fucking glad to see you guys." Asher sighed, and as soon as I moved away from my place wedged in between them, he rushed at them too with his arms open wide for a bro hug.

Adler held his hand up, and a thick wall of rock sprouted from the stones that made up the floor and stopped him in his tracks.

A broken look flashed across Asher's eyes, and the smile dropped from his face.

I had to remind myself that I hated him because the look in his eyes hurt my heart.

Something strange was going on, and I had to figure it out, and fast, before the outside world burned down by whoever the hell it was.

My first thought was twins. Could he have had one? But I quickly ruled it out. The guys would have known that.

As far as I knew, all he had was a sister that used to date Apollo.

And this was no chick standing in front of me.

He had the same dark red hair and sharp jawline, dotted with a scruffy beard. If that wasn't enough to convince me he was a dude, the muscles that rippled underneath his shirt were.

But by the looks on everyone's faces, they were all just as confused- except for Silas.

He sat perched in the window with a smirk on his face. He looked more like he was watching the latest episode of his favorite soap opera, not watching everything I thought I knew crumble before my eyes.

I almost wanted to ask him if he wanted a fucking bowl of popcorn for his show, but I was afraid that he'd say yes.

Asher sighed and dropped his hands down by his sides. "Look, guys. I don't have the slightest fucking clue of what's going on here, okay? Obviously, I'm missing a few of the details because Apollo tried to kill me, you practically tried to spear me with a fucking rock wall, and this fire mage freed me. I'm missing a hell of a lot of pieces."

"She's not a fire mage, actually." Silas finally decided to chime in. "She's an eden."

"Which you already knew," I said with a raised brow. "You knew that because you tried to kill me. On more than one occasion, actually." I reminded.

I didn't know how it would be possible to forget someone that you'd been trying to commit homicide on for days.

I was slightly offended if I was honest. Was I really that forgettable?

"What? Why the hell would I do that?" Asher shook his head.

"No. I don't have any idea what's going on, but I know I wouldn't do that. Try to kill a complete stranger? Why?"

"That's what I've been asking myself since the moment you showed up, fucked my best friend, burned my house to the ground, and almost drove me insane," I said through gritted teeth. I could finally feel it, the small spurts of anger coming back to me, which was good. I needed it.

I needed to be fierce. I couldn't let him think that whatever trick he was trying to pull on me was working.

I was sure the second I let my guard down. He would pounce, try to kill me, and probably burn Silas's entire realm down too.

I didn't put anything past Asher at that point. I had learned my lesson too many times.

But Asher shook his head, an explosive laugh erupting from his lungs.

He laughed so loud and so hard that it took everyone by surprise.

We all exchanged anxious looks. We had just gone through hell to get there, to find the missing pieces of the puzzle, but all that had happened was more being added.

"I don't know who you're talking about, but it's not me." He shook his head, furiously.

The scary part wasn't the laugh or his insistence on not knowing a single thing. Hell, I wasn't even scared that he was there in the first place.

The scary thing, the part that sunk into my bones and rocked me with a fear that I couldn't understand, was that I believed him.

Chapter Two

"You stay right here." I pushed Asher gently into the back corner and spun him around to face the wall like a toddler who was put into time out. "We need to have a meeting."

"Are you serious?" Asher sighed and crossed his arms.

"Or I could just let Apollo take another crack at you." I raised a brow.

Asher huffed. He didn't say a word, but he stayed in his place in the corner.

I grabbed Silas by the arm, and a devilishly sexy grin spread across his lips. "Finally? I get to join the fun?" His accent was thick.

"Yes. You stand here and watch him. So much fun. You're welcome." I said, pulling him beside me and placing him directly behind Asher.

"Now, make sure he doesn't move."

"And what am I supposed to do if he does?"

"Idk, time him to death or something? What's the use of being able to manipulate time if you can't use it for anything?" I teased.

"The answer is I do not know."

I rolled my eyes and strolled back across the room.

The sounds from down the hallway seemed to be getting closer and closer. The kingdom was waking up, and I didn't know how the hell they'd react to a bunch of strangers somehow appearing there. Not to mention the sudden appearance of their long lost king- or supposed to be king?

I didn't know exactly how to describe the utterly complicated royalty situation that Silas had told me.

But I knew that we needed to figure out a plan, and we needed to do it quickly.

I may not have known Asher very well, but I knew Apollo, and he could only play nice for so long.

I felt like a teacher trying to keep the kids from killing each other during recess.

I huddled up with the guys like we were on a football team, trying to develop a play.

"Does anyone know what the fuck is going on?" I whispered, a lot louder than I probably should have, but I didn't really care.

"Not a clue. But that's pretty much every day for me." Adler laughed.

I couldn't help but laugh too. Even in the most fucked up situations, Adler wasn't afraid to crack a joke or smile, and it made me feel brave enough to do it too.

It definitely made the situation feel a lot better.

Even Atlas cracked a smile.

But Apollo, on the other hand, was the most serious that I'd ever seen him.

Something was going on with him. I could feel it. He was so deeply enraged about something. It was there underneath the surface. I wanted to ask him what about seeing Asher was so triggering to him, but I knew he wouldn't tell me anyway.

He might not have ever told me, but I knew there was less of a chance of him opening up in a room full of testosterone.

My only bet was to separate him from the others and pry later.

But right now, we had a situation on our hands.

"I believe him." The words spilled out of Apollo's lips like water before I even had time to ask a question.

"Wait. What?" My head snapped in his direction almost faster than my vertebrae would let me.

"I said, I believe him." Apollo said, his voice flat and unwavering.

A silence fell over the group as we all processed what he was saying.

No one was expecting it. I could tell by the way that the other's eyes widened.

Apollo was literally just trying to kill him. If I hadn't stopped him, he probably would have sliced him in half. He knew how to make his water whip dangerously sharp. I didn't doubt it.

"Why?" Atlas asked the question that was on everyone's mind.

"Look at his face." Was the only explanation that Apollo dared to give. But it was the only explanation that the others needed.

I, on the other hand, had no idea what his face had to do with anything.

"Hey, Asher." Adler called.

Asher turned around and looked at us for a split second before he spun back around.

"Holy shit, you're right."

"I see it now too." Atlas chimed in, once again leaving me in the dust.

"Can someone please fill me in? Or are we all talking in code?" I sighed.

"He's missing his scar, the one through his eye," Adler said calmly. "Apollo here gave it to him a long time ago because-"

"Why he got it doesn't matter." Apollo barked so quickly that I flinched.

He was touchy, a lot more than usual. Something was eating away at him.

And now I knew that it had to do with the scar.

But why?

"The point is that he doesn't have it. So I don't know if he's a fucking clone or some weird time-warped version of him, but I believe him when he says he doesn't know what's going on. He couldn't possibly because everything happened after he got that scar. That was when the shit show started." Apollo's fist clenched tightly at his side, and the tension radiated off of him like a heater.

It was so thick you could cut it with a water whip.

"Okay," I said, drawing the word out a little longer than usual to give myself time to process what the hell was happening. "So we agree, we believe him. He doesn't know what's going on or why everyone hates him. But we need to figure out why. What the hell is going on?"

Everyone nodded, but nobody had a single thing to go off of. It was like we hit a brick wall. We were at a dead-end. All the information came to a screeching halt.

Then Silas spun around.

"If I may speak love?" He flashed his signature, charming smile. "I think I may have a way to find the answers that you're seeking."

***

"Are you freaking serious?" My voice was hardly a whisper as I crept down the empty hall behind Silas. "You had information this entire freaking time, and you chose to watch us go at each other like wild dogs instead of speaking up?"

"Why would I speak up when your confused face was so cute?" He turned around and paused just to wink at me.

I could almost feel Apollo grunt from behind me.

I was surprised that he agreed to share me at all. He definitely wasn't very good at it. But I gave him an A for effort.

I had to admit. I had feelings for each of the guys- Silas included. I could never pick just one.

Apollo understood that.

It didn't mean he loved it, but he understood it.

I nudged Silas forward, digging the palm of my hand into his back, and he crept forward once again, carefully.

Now that the kingdom was awake again, he was careful.

I didn't know what he was afraid of or why he was hiding, but he had information that we needed. I didn't see much more of a choice than to play the game by his rules.

We slowly crept forward, sure to stay in the shadows.

A few muddled voices came from somewhere out in the corridor that the hallway opened up to.

It sounded like two women. They shared the same British sounding accent that Silas had, so I had to listen a little more intently to fully pick up their conversation as we neared the end of the hallway.

"And the prince just disappeared?" One of them said to the other.

"I don't know. That's what they're saying. No one has the slightest clue what's gone on. He was here a moment and gone the next."

It didn't take a rocket scientist to know that they were talking about Silas.

I vaguely remembered that he had said something about his coronation and how he had missed it, but in my defense, I was under a lot of pressure, and it was easy to forget details. I couldn't quite remember the whole story.

But I remembered that he had said that he was trying to erase a fire mage from the timeline before everything went to shit.

It had to be Asher, right? What other fire mage was on the loose trying to destroy the world as we knew it?

But I knew we were there now, and his kingdom wasn't frozen anymore. Hell, the citizens were practically begging for him back.

But he chose to hide in the shadows instead.

Strange.

When we got to the end of the hallway, we paused and waited for the two women to venture off further into the castle before we dared cross the open space and book it for the stairs.

We all crept toward them and hurried up to the second floor of the castle.

There was some sort of commotion outside the castle walls. I could hear it even from inside its thick walls of rock.

But I didn't dare say a thing. It was probably the reason we could even move so freely around the castle. I figured being frozen was enough to rile any group of people up, not to mention being frozen and having a missing prince.

We got to the top floor, and Silas peaked around the corner before whipping his head back around quickly.

"One moment please." He held up a finger.

And before I could even say a word, a flash of light erupted in front of me, and Silas disappeared.

"I forgot he could do that." I whispered to myself.

I turned to the others who stood behind me, all looking at me questioningly.

Asher stood between Adler and Atlas near the back. They had been the appointed lookouts to keep an eye on Asher. None of us trusted Apollo as far as we could throw him.

Nobody knew when the next time he was going to snap. We all knew it was coming. It was the when part that was the mystery.

I stood quietly, but my brain was thinking louder than it ever had. It was like the further we got into trying to unravel the mystery that was my life, the more tangles we found, not only in it but in the entire universe.

Time.

Who knew that time was an element? One to be manipulated?

All I knew was that the old Eden, the one who worked at the coffee shop and let people walk all over her, would have never seen any of it coming. It wasn't even feasible in her mind.

A slight smile graced my lips at the thought of how much I'd grown from the person I was. How much I'd evolved.

How much stronger I was.

There wasn't a doubt in my mind that the old Eden would love me, the new and improved version.

The stronger version.

The version that saw Apollo, a big, burly water mage charging right at her out of anger and stood her ground with her head held high instead of cowering beneath the pressure.

A sound of grunting and thudding came from further down the

hallway, around the corner, and pulled me from the murky depths of my thoughts.

Metal clashed against a hard surface, and then it was quiet.

I knew I wasn't supposed to, but I peeked around the corner again, just in time to see a broad set of bright red doors at the end, two unconscious guards in full armor on the ground, and Silas standing in the open doorway with a smirk on his face.

"Don't worry. They're merely unconscious." He smiled as I made my way to him.

I just rolled my eyes, but I was secretly impressed that he could take out two large guards on his own.

He wasn't the most buff guy around.

I passed him and stepped into the dimly lit room.

"What exactly are we doing-" My words trailed off the minute my eyes laid on what was ahead. In a large glass chest, sitting on a glowing podium, was a large sand clock.

Chapter Three

"What the hell is that?" Apollo's jaw hung open as he stumbled into the room.

"And why is it glowing like a fucking disco ball?" Adler threw the comment in as soon as his eyes landed on the thing.

I didn't know what to say. If I was honest, after everything that had happened, I nearly forgot about the timeclock all together. Silas had told me about it, but when I saw Asher tumble out of that doorway it was like every coherent thought in my mind stumbled out of it too- and straight off of a cliff.

The second my eyes found the clock, it was impossible to rip them away.

It sat so proudly in the glass case, it was almost impossible not to look at.

The room itself was bare. Nothing hung on the walls, and there weren't any doors besides the ones we had entered in. Everything about it, including the soft lighting that shone down on it, seemed like it was built to house the clock.

There was something special about that, something sacred. Even the air felt different, more pure, maybe even still.

But none of it could compare to the energy that radiated off the clock. It was like a power source, and the vibes were just pouring out, washing over me, calling my name.

It was like it was made for me.

But out of all of us, none seemed more in awe than Asher.

He stood at the back of the room, his eyes like two big saucers, soaking in every drop of the clock that they could. There was a sparkle there too. Something was lingering just below the surface.

"This isn't the sand clock of time, is it?" He said with an amazed smirk. "It can't be. I didn't actually think it existed."

I was surprised that he knew what it was when the others seemed utterly lost.

But then his facial expression dropped as his mind started putting two and two together.

"Wait a minute." He turned to Silas, with his eyes wide. "Wait a goddamn minute! Is this the Realm of Time? It is, isn't it!"

"What the hell do you know about the Realm of Time?" Apollo threw an ugly look in his direction.

"A lot more than you, I'm guessing."

My mouth dropped open at the fighting words slung so carelessly at a hothead like Apollo. I couldn't tell if Asher was just stupid and didn't remember the self-destructive tendencies that the water mage had, or if he just didn't care.

Either way, when Apollo rushed at him, knocked him to the ground, and his fist connected with the side of his jaw, I saw it coming from a mile away.

I didn't want to be an *I told you so* type of person, but when Adler and Atlas ripped him off of Asher, I had to hold the words in.

He should have known better than to poke the bear.

"Are you boys done playing yet?" I said instead and made my way to the middle of the room.

The closer I got to the glass class the more I realized that the large clock didn't hold sand. It contained some other shimmering particles that sifted inside its glass confines.

Glitter maybe?

I squinted to try to get a better look. Whatever it was, the shimmering was one of the most beautiful things that I'd ever seen, and that was coming from someone who had rejected all things pink, fuzzy, and glittery for her entire life.

There was a flash of light, and, as the guys behind me sorted each other out as guys do, Silas appeared beside me.

"They're realities, love."

I looked up at him, confusion etched into the lines on my forehead as my brows pulled together.

"The particles. I can tell you're trying to figure out what they are, they're realities. Every tiny particle is a different reality. A different version of the world where you and I are walking around, living our lives in different ways, each more so than the last."

I blinked a few times before tearing my eyes from his and letting them land back on the clock.

If what he was saying was right, there was no telling how many different realities the thing held. Easily thousands, if not millions.

The clock itself wasn't much bigger than two of my hands stacked on top of each other, but the twinkle of the particles told me they were small. It wouldn't be hard to cram a million inside.

I didn't know exactly what to say, or why he brought me there, or even what the hell I was supposed to do next.

But seeing those particles and knowing that the clock was filled with millions of other Eden's walking around in their lives, not knowing what the hell was going on made me feel a little bit better.

Who knew, maybe one of them was actually getting something right.

God knew that it wasn't me, though.

I took a deep breath and closed my eyes as the sound of another fistfight starting behind me filled the room.

I tried to imagine that it was me. I was the reality where I got it right. Maybe I just didn't know it yet.

Because the truth is, nobody knows what they're doing. We're all walking around our lives, cluelessly making choices and hoping for the best. Every day we wake up, we live another day of life that we'd never lived before, and as big and scary as that is, it's for a reason.

I knew I just had to find mine.

I opened my eyes and spun around, a new fire born in the pit of my stomach, motivating me in ways that I'd never felt before.

"Stop it. All of you!" I said so firmly that it caught all of the guys by surprise at once.

They all froze where they stood, Adler holding back Apollo and Atlas holding back Asher.

"I'm sorry, I thought I was here with the best elemental mages that time has ever known. Not a bunch of toddlers who want to fight at recess." I said in a tone so calm that it almost scared me.

"Now you guys can fight all you want, hell you can kill each other for all I care, but what you're not about to do is do it on my time. I don't know if you guys forgot, but outside these walls, there's a pyromaniac homicidal mage destroying the castes. He's hurting innocent people and tearing life as we know it to threads. It won't be long before he starts an all-out war between all the elements , and the entire country destroys itself from the inside out."

The guys slowly straightened up, all looking like sad puppies that just got yelled at by their owner.

"You can kill each other, but so help me God, you will not do it until we figure out what the hell is going on and how we can stop it. Do you hear me?" I used my best mom voice. I didn't remember ever having one, but I'd watched enough television to fake it.

And by the fear that quaked in their eyes, I knew that if I ever had kids, they were toast.

"I said, do you understand?" I cocked my head to the sighed, and the guys all groaned in agreement, all of their eyes managing to snap in different directions to avoid direct contact with mine.

It was okay though. I didn't need them to look me in the eyes.

What I did need them to do was stop sabotaging our mission before we even really knew what it was.

And I think I got that point through pretty well, judging by the way they all sulked to opposite corners of the room.

"Kids." Silas groaned with a sarcastic smirk as I turned my attention back to the chest in the middle of the room.

"The worst." I rolled my eyes before smiling back.

My eyes fixated on the clock once again, and I remembered what Silas had told me about its power.

Something about it, giving the wielder the power to fix the timeline and change things in the past.

But I also remembered his explicit warning not to do it and how all it took was a single misstep to change the entire course of reality.

So why had he marched me right inside and stood me in front of it?

What was his endgame?

I turned to look at him, and he arched a purple brow, almost like he already knew what I was wondering, where my mind was.

The thing about Silas was that he basically was a mystery, and I mean that in the most poetic way possible.

Everything about him, from the way he spoke to the way he

looked, all the way down to the way he acted, felt like one big riddle.

I felt like I was so close to the answers that I had been searching for my whole life. They were there, right across the bridge, but Silas was the troll standing in between me and my destiny, and he wouldn't let me pass until I solved his riddle.

But what the hell his riddle was, was a mystery just as big to me.

I tore my eyes from him and back to the container that held the clock before I realized that it was all one cohesive piece of glass. There were no sharp corners, only curves. There was no top or bottom. You couldn't even tell where it started or where it ended. Sure, it was in the shape of a treasure chest, but there was no keyhole or even a hinge for it to open up.

It was just a glass chamber that held the clock hostage.

I reached out to tap my knuckle lightly against it, but my hand met a shimmering purple forcefield that was wrapped around it. The second my knuckle touched it, waves of energy rippled throughout it, revealing that the mystical forcefield covered the entire thing.

"What the hell? How are we supposed to get to the clock?"

"That's the question, isn't it?" Silas sighed. His tone was his typical, chipper one, but I could tell that there was a layer of frustration behind it.

"A super-powerful weapon that we can't even use. That makes a lot of sense. Why did you even bring us here?" Adler sighed.

"From my experience, when weapons are locked away, it's usually so no one can use them, dipshit." Apollo barked in his direction and nursed the sore spot on his jaw, where Asher must have clocked him.

There was a moment of silence, and the look on Adler's face nearly broke me.

I was about to walk over and sock Apollo once too for being a dick to someone who most definitely did not deserve it. But as soon as the words left his mouth Apollo did something that he seldom did- regretted them.

It was written all over his face, and even though I knew it hurt him to do, he let out a sigh and apologized.

"Hey man, I'm sorry. I didn't mean that."

The words almost sounded foreign coming from his mouth.

Stone cold apollo. The guy that never let anyone in, realized that he might want to keep the very few friends he had?

That was a new one.

Something about being in Asher's presence changed Apollo in a handful of different ways that I knew went beyond old friends turning into enemies. There was more to the story, probably a lot more.

But unfortunately for me, I didn't have that kind of time to stroll down memory lane.

"So we need to figure out how to open this thing so-" My words were cut off by an immediate shrieking voice.

A maid carrying a pot of water had noticed the guards lying unconscious in the hallway and had poked her head inside the room in enough time to see Silas standing.

"The prince!" She screamed down the hall. "The Prince! The

prince has returned!"

Before we knew what was going on, an entire group of people flooded in from the halls, rushing so fast that they had to skid to a stop.

Then came the whisking. People grabbed us in excitement and whisked us in all different directions chanting in happiness at the return of their long lost prince.

While Silas, on the other hand, looked like he might throw up.

Well fuck.

Chapter Four

W e were all being pushed and prodded by the excited locals and herded out of the room like cattle. At one point, I noticed the look in Apollo's eyes. The same one that he got every time he was about to lose control.

I didn't know what the hell made him so angry all the time, what trauma had caused it, but at that moment, I was a few seconds away from shattering the glass, grabbing the sand clock, and obliterating it from his timeline. Partly because it was rough walking around with the magical equivalent of a stick of dynamite with its own mind, but also because I could tell he was really hurting.

As much as he hated to show it, and as much as I hated to admit that I knew, he had feelings.

A lot of them, in fact.

I remembered rolling over his body in bed, his skin brushing up against mine. I remembered feeling him in every way known to man, buried deep inside my most sacred place- the first person ever to venture there.

We had a connection, one that he liked to deny a lot of times, but we did.

And when he hurt, I hurt too.

Unfortunately for both of us, that was all the time.

"Apollo! Cool it!" I yelled over the excited shouts of the townspeople.

I watched his eyes dart up to mine, and he slid the steam of water back into his pouch.

I glanced at all the guys, being whisked in different directions, and ultimately on Silas.

I was surprised that he hadn't just pulled his famous disappearing act.

But there was something about him, too, that changed. It was like when he was with us, he was a mysterious stranger, with no place to call home, just drifting through.

But the second that they called him their prince, it was almost like I could physically see the weight of his world land back on his shoulders.

I had to decide on who to follow before I too was channeled to a random wing of the castle, and I knew in my soul that Apollo was the one who needed me most.

If anything, Atlas and Adler could charm their way out of any situation, and they both were holding on to Asher for dear life.

It was Apollo that I was worried about. He was like a dog. You never knew when he was going to bite.

And I had to make sure I was there if he did.

"Excuse me. Excuse me!" I shouted, shoving through the crowd, dodging unsolicited hugs from people I'd never known a day in my life.

I had never seen a group of people so happy in my life, their smiles shone bright, and their eyes were bright enough to match too.

They truly were happy to see Silas, but why didn't his smile match?

What was it about his kingdom that he was running from?

And why did I have a feeling that it had something to do with the sand clock, and even worse, me?

I finally made my way to Apollo and grabbed onto the sleeve of his shirt, dodging another unwelcome hug.

His head turned so fast that it nearly spun around, and there was an angry look in his eyes until he realized it was me who had latched on to him.

Apollo was never the type of person who liked affection and hugs. Atlas and Adler? Hell yes. Atlas had kissed me the second he met me.

But Apollo went out of his way to avoid it.

I think it reminded him of all the things he was trying to shut out from his life.

"Hey, it's me," I said, my eyes locking on to his. "I'll come with you."

I wanted to say a million more things, and more importantly, I wanted to tell him that no matter what demons from his past, he was battling that it was okay, but instead, I just nodded.

I knew that he knew what I meant.

But in a crowd full of strangers wasn't the time for me to yell out everything that I thought he needed to hear.

"The prince is back!" The crowd all chanted. "To the guest chambers with all of his guests! There will be a feast!"

At some point during the commotion, a group of people with strange, medieval-sounding instruments appeared and started to play a tune.

Just like that the mob became a party, dancing and swaying down the hallway, their bodies colliding with ours and bumping us in the direction of what I guessed was the guest chambers.

For a realm that was practically a little pocket inside space and time, they all dressed fairly old fashioned with long dresses and old-style clothing. The women wore their hair down in loose curls with jewels and other glittering objects fastened inside their hair, and each person had a brightly colored tone. There wasn't a brown, or blonde, or even a redhead in sight. They had bright blues, oranges, and even pinks that seemed to grow naturally like that.

Silas's bright purple shade made a little more sense when I saw the other people in the kingdom.

I wondered if they all had an affinity for teleporting and

controlling time like in our world, everyone could control an element.

But as I glanced back, I saw Silas all the way down the hall, being brought around a corner, and knew it was a question that I'd have to wait to ask.

Finally, we got to the opposite end of the hall, turned the corner, and a row of doors lined both sides.

They stopped at the first one, opened the door, and ushered Apollo inside.

I tried to follow him, but one of the women tried to stop me. "We have separate quarters for you, ma'am." She said, her accent light and fluttery.

"Oh no, I have to go with him," I said all too quickly.

"But-"

"I have to."

She looked at a blue-haired girl that stood beside her, and they both raised their perfectly groomed brows with a knowing look.

"Okay." She winked at me before shoving me inside and closing the door.

I turned back to the closed door.

"No, it's not like that!" I yelled defiantly.

"Don't worry. We'll make sure you and your husband aren't disturbed." One of them yelled back before they both giggled and scurried away to catch up to the crowd that had gotten away from them.

I spun around, let out a sigh, and slid to the floor with my back pressed against the wall.

Apollo stood in front of me with both hands lodged in his pockets, as casual as ever as if he wasn't just about to kill all of those people on an angry whim.

"Oh, husband?" He smirked. "So, that's what you call me behind my back?"

"Oh shove it." I huffed. "I'd call you my grandad if it got me into the room to keep you from self-destructing."

Apollo rolled his eyes and turned away from me, pretending he was suddenly super interested in the room's architecture.

Inside was a king-sized bed with an enchantingly beautiful canopy overhead, with a sheer pink cloth encasing all sides of it. Across the room, a large armoire stood tall, pressed up against the stone wall. There was a single window carved into the farthest wall, which was about it, the entire thing lit by candlelight and sunlight.

It made me wonder what year it was for them. Were they going to be stuck without technology forever, or was it a choice?

You'd think a society that could manipulate time would have picked an era that was a little more advanced.

Or did they know something that we didn't about what it took to be happy and thrive?

Of course, Apollo went straight to the window and gazed out, back to his normal brooding self.

"What are you doing?" I got up from my place on the floor and brushed myself off.

"Finding a way out, what does it look like?" He refused to look back at me.

"Well, if you really want to know, it looks like you're heavily trying to outrun your emotions and overcompensate for them with anger because it's the only emotion you're comfortable feeling."

The words just fell from my lips. I hadn't planned to bust him out like that and throw everything on the table, but he had asked me.

I wasn't going to lie to him.

His head whipped around in my direction, but I casually strolled to the armoire and pretended like everything was fine.

I pulled the doors open and gazed at the fine clothes inside, politely ignoring the holes he was burning into the back of my head with his eyes.

I was glad it was Asher that had the firepower and not Apollo. From what I gathered from the guys, it was the fire that drove Asher mad.

It was something different with Apollo. His emotions were the only blazing force that he needed control of. The fire would have pushed him over the edge, and we would have had a force far greater than Asher to reckon with.

"What do you know." Apollo grumbled.

I ran my fingertips over the smooth fabric of the shirts and dresses that were hung inside, all vibrant colors, almost bright enough to match the people's hair shades.

"A lot." I turned around, as nonchalant as I could, and faced him with a stone-cold gaze.

"Yeah, right."

I didn't know exactly why, but his words rubbed me raw in a way that I didn't see coming- insulted me almost.

"You don't think I know what it's like to be hurting?" My words came out hot and laced with anger. "To lash out every chance that I got?"

"What are you talking about? You were a timid little thing before I found you?"

He didn't know it, but he almost signed his own death certificate with those words.

"Oh, because I wasn't a fucking tornado that ripped through everything and everyone around me every time that I got angry means that I didn't feel pain? Because I wasn't the human form of a volcano that was waiting for someone to give me a reason to erupt, I don't know what it's like to feel lonely?"

Apollo opened his mouth to say something, but I held up a finger, and he clamped it closed, recognizing the fire in my eyes because he knew it was the same fire that he held in his every single day too.

"At least you got to know your family before you were put to sleep for a century. At least you got to learn to hone your powers, and meet people, and feel love, and fall in love."

The words slipped from my mouth before I could stop them, and suddenly, it was all out in the open. He knew that I knew about Asher's sister and the moments that they shared. It was all out on the table.

And the hurt in his eyes was hard to see. But if I could see it, that meant his walls were going down, and I knew that I couldn't stop.

I was so close to getting through to him and figuring out the real reason he was on a warpath.

"I know what heartbreak feels like, too, remember?" I sighed and made my way to the bed.

I moved the sheer curtain to the side and plopped down on the end of it.

"Just because I wasn't in love with Jade doesn't mean I didn't love her. It's a different kind of love, but it's love nonetheless. And she isn't dead, but the version of her that I knew is, and that stings."

Apollo stopped and thought for a moment. I could almost see him wrestling with himself inside his mind before he let out a long sigh and made his way to the bed beside me too.

"You know?" He looked up at me, and I could see the tears that dotted his waterline, threatening to escape with any blink.

"More than I want to, but not as much as I need to." I groaned.

Apollo looked away, focusing on a far off point across the room.

"It just fucking hurts, you know?" His voice didn't waver, but the tears made their way down his cheeks. "It just hurts."

I believed him. I knew it did because if it hurt as much as it hurt me to see him like that, it was a hell of a lot.

"So, share it with me." I said, my voice soft.

My fingertips found his tear-stained chin, and turned his face back in my direction.

"What?"

"I said, share it with me." I leaned in a little closer, closing in the space between us, my eyes focusing on his lips. "We can hurt together."

I pulled him close, my lips locked onto his, and everything else fell to the wayside.

Chapter Five

The second our lips touched, an electric wave of energy swept through me and went into him. I could tell that he felt it too by the way he jumped backward, pulling away from our kiss.

It was something about our chemistry but knew it was more than that. We had sparked, just like I had with the rest of the guys, and each of them brought out a different type of power in me. They seemed to summon something from deep inside of me and pull it to the surface like a beast waiting to be tamed.

And who better to take charge and try to tame it than Apollo. It was basically written into his genes to be dominant, and who didn't like to be dominated every now and then?

There was a questioning look in his eye, but it was mixed in with something else, a rabid lust that I knew was taking over his body. It was easy to tell by the bulge that grew in his pants.

He thought for a moment, and that was all it took for him to decide that taking me was worth it.

I knew it was driving him crazy, seeing everyone else get a share of me before he got to get his fill again.

The truth was when we'd first had sex, it was all new to me. I was practically a different person, but now I was ready to show him what I was capable of.

Ready to let him devour every inch of my body, his anger, and all.

Because maybe all he needed was someone he could call his. Maybe years of being tucked away and hidden and degraded the part of him that craved human interaction.

I didn't care if I had to fuck him a hundred times to wake it back up. It was time well spent.

He threw caution to the wind and came back in for another kiss with so much force that it knocked me on my back, my body sinking into the plush mattress.

I giggled as he crawled on top of me and pinned my wrists to the bed.

"You, Eden Montgomery, drive me fucking crazy." He said with a primal growl, his lips only inches from mine.

"You love it, though," I smirked.

His lips came crashing into mine in a sloppy passionate kiss, almost before I could finish my sentence.

Butterflies bubbled up in my stomach, being resurrected from a time that felt so long ago.

The weight of his body pressed into mine, and I opened my legs to let him settle between them, his erection grinding against my clit beneath our clothes.

Mid kiss, I sunk my teeth into his bottom lip, a little harder than I should have, simply to annoy him.

I preached at the guys not to poke the angry bear, and there I was beneath his weight, agitating him for sexual fun.

Some role model I was.

He pulled away from me and dabbed at his lip with his fingertip, a small dot of blood coming off.

"Oops, did I do that?" I smirked.

He smirked too, and a different kind of look crossed his eyes: one that I hadn't seen before, a new, playful type of anger.

"Oh, it's going to be like that, huh?" He smirked and went back in for another kiss, this time he sunk his teeth into my bottom lip, a lot gentler than I knew I deserved after I nearly ripped his off, but it sent a rush of adrenaline through my body nonetheless. It started at the top of my head and radiated all the way down into my clit, leaving nothing but a dull ache, my body begging to feel his bare skin against mine.

His lips migrated from mine, down to my jaw, and then my neck, where he sunk his teeth into my skin again.

"Say it." I moaned.

"Say what?" His voice was nearly a whisper, and I could feel his hot breath against my skin.

"That you love it." I moaned. "My craziness."

He came back up from my neck and looked me in my eyes with a seriousness that I hadn't seen in a long time.

Then he said something that I definitely wasn't expecting. "Fuck your craziness. I love you."

I stared up at him blankly, my mind running a million miles a minute to try to process what he had just said. My stomach felt five different kinds of butterflies jumping around inside of it wildly, and every inch of my skin tingled like it was asleep.

Me.

After Apollo was reminded of someone he once cared for, and I'm sure his soul felt like it was ripped from his body, it was me that he loved.

Years after what he had thought was his greatest love was taken from him, it was me that he chose.

Me.

The pushover from the coffee shop that hated his guts for a significant portion of the time that we had known each other.

Me.

And the crazy part was I felt it too, every single ounce of the wildly burning, passionate, sometimes toxic feeling love that crept into my bones and made my body its home. The love that made my heart swell and my stomach ache.

A love that I had always wished that I would feel, but now that I did, it seemed big, scary, and a little bit intimidating.

Those were all things that would have stopped the old version of me from even coming close to it. I wouldn't have touched passion like that with a ten-foot pole. I valued feeling safe over feeling seen.

Now, I said fuck that.

"I love you too." I replied.

My voice was soft, nearly a whisper, but there was no doubt in my mind that he heard it because the way he pulled me in for a kiss was different this time.

It was less filled with lust and more filled with a passion that radiated off of him. It was infectious, and I felt it creep into my mouth from his kiss, crawl its way down my throat, and settle in the pit of my stomach.

He loved me, and I loved him.

In a world filled with mystical elements and magical sand clocks, something as complicated as that suddenly seemed simple.

It didn't mean how many other people I loved too, how many of the guys I shared a piece of my soul with, it didn't make my love for the others burn any less bright.

And at that moment, the love I had for him was burning the brightest that it ever had.

I got lost in our kiss and melted into him like butter spread on warm toast. His hands roamed my body underneath my shirt, and mine found their way behind his head to tangle my fingers in his blue locks.

It was more than just a makeout session. It was a spiritual act.

I didn't doubt that for a second. It was like our bodies meshed together, and the longer we laid there, the harder it was for me to tell where his body ended and where mine began.

And the less I wanted to.

He peeled my clothes off slowly, with a fire in his eyes.

He understood exactly what he was doing to me. He knew how wet I was, how I wanted nothing more than to feel him stuff himself inside of me, and that was exactly why he took his time.

He tossed my clothes on the floor beside the bed, leaving me in nothing but my panties and bra, before gazing upon my body. His eyes hungrily ate up every inch of me, and I let them.

Satisfied with his view, I felt him slide a finger underneath the waistband of my panties and slowly pull them down the length of my legs, tantalizing me with every inch until they joined the rest of my clothes in a crumpled heap on the ground.

He wedged his warm hands in between my thighs and opened my legs wide, spreading my pussy just for him. There I was, on full display, my lips glistening wet, waiting for him.

Without saying a word, Apollo leaned in and brought his mouth to my love spot, flicking my clit with his tongue.

I moaned and bucked my hips against his face, but he placed a hand firmly on my lower stomach and held me still, in the perfect position for him to taste every part of my pussy.

Pleasure washed over me in waves, and my eyes rolled back into my head.

He ate me out like I was the best thing he'd ever tasted, like it was his last meal, and he wanted to remember the sweet taste of my lips.

He ran his tongue up and down the length of me until I felt two of his fingers glide inside smoothly, stretching me out just enough.

Another moan escaped my lips, my eyes still closed, until I felt his freehand leave my stomach and slide underneath the back of my head.

He tilted my head to point right at him and moaned underneath his breath.

"Open your eyes. I want you to watch me claim every part of you. I don't care how many people I have to share you with, right now, you're mine."

The gruff, primal growl of his voice alone made me open my eyes, and they landed on his.

I watched as he devoured me, moans escaping my lips uncontrollably as he finger fucked me.

Right before I was about to cum he pulled his fingers out, slid me off my back, and placed me on my knees in front of him.

I barely had enough time to process what was going on before he slid his monster of a cock inside of my mouth, and it slid all the way to the back of my throat.

I wrapped my fingers around the base of his dick and moved my head and hand in tandem, jacking him off while I sucked his soul out of his dick.

I loved that I could feel it still growing inside of my mouth. The harder I sucked, the harder he got.

His hand held firmly to the back of my head as he slightly thrust in and out of my throat.

He was getting close, I could feel it, and I challenged myself to go faster and try to make him cum before he had the chance to shove his cock into my pussy, for no other reason than to annoy him.

I sucked him off faster, and I felt him twitch.

"Hey." He moaned. "Slow down."

I half smirked as I kept my pace, and I could feel him on the brink.

I almost did it, almost made him bust when he pulled me up from the ground, flipped me on my stomach, and bent me over the bed before ramming his cock into me at full force.

I yelped, the pleasure and pain hitting me at the same time.

"Nice try." He moaned before pulling his cock all the way out and shoving it back inside, pressing against my G-spot. "Out there, you might be in charge, but in here, I am."

My clit quivered at his words, and that was it.

My clit tingled, and my mind exploded with pleasure, my pussy clamping down on his cock, massaging it perfectly.

I felt him thrust one final time and a gush of his warm cum shoot out and fill me up.

It was the best feeling ever.

He pulled out with a smile on his face, and I collapsed on the bed before he crawled on beside me and kissed my forehead.

"I needed that." He whispered thankfully.

"I know." I smiled, my chest still heaving. "Me too."

Chapter Six

I fought my eyes, begging them to stay open despite how comfortable the bed was, enchantingly comfortable actually.

I was so entranced by its soft touch that I didn't even bother putting my clothes back on, something that Apollo didn't seem to mind for a single second.

He glanced over at me, raw and exposed on the bed, every so often as he slipped his clothes back on.

He seemed lighter, less harsh. I didn't get the feeling like he wanted to kill everyone in any room that he would walk into anymore, which was a good sign.

Especially for a hothead like him.

The anger was still there, accompanied by the mysterious hurt, but it was softer at the edges- less lethal.

I watched, slightly disappointed that his washboard abs had to go back into their hiding place underneath his shirt.

I was a firm believer that works of art like that should be shared with the world.

I pulled back the blanket and slipped into the warm embrace of the covers.

"You're really making yourself at home here, aren't you? We should be worried about finding Asher and figuring out what the hell he's up to." Asher groaned.

There it was, the edge was coming back, and I had a feeling it was coming with a vengeance.

"I'm not worried about that right now," I said as calmly as I could, both because I was trying to keep my composure and because I was on the verge of falling asleep.

I wasn't entirely sure what I had done that was so exhausting, but whatever it was, it wiped out most of my power.

I knew if Apollo got anywhere near Asher again before I had time to sort out what was going on inside that handsomely brooding head of his, it would just be meltdown central.

And I didn't know if I had the energy to stop him this time.

"Hey," I called out, but this time I used my *listen to me* tone, and he noticed.

He zipped up his pants and looked at me.

"Lay with me. Please?" I batted my lashes like a cartoon

character and tried to caress the bed beside me seductively.

"Only if you promise never to do anything as cringey as that again." A stifled laugh fell from his lips, but he sulked his way to the bed and laid down on top of the blankets.

Ouch.

"Oh, come on." I groaned, pulling the blankets out from underneath him. "Underneath the blankets. At least pretend like you're putting in the effort." I tossed them back on top of him with a satisfied smile and scooted closer to him.

Neither one of us was much for affection, and we definitely weren't the cuddling type, but something told me that he needed it.

We both did.

"There. Was that so hard?" I jabbed him in the rib cage with my elbow before laying my head on his shoulder.

"Very." Apollo laughed.

A silence fell over the room, and after a few awkward seconds of him trying to figure out what to do, he wrapped his arm around my shoulders and tucked his hand behind his head.

His heartbeat slowly in his chest, in a thudding rhythm that almost lulled me to sleep.

But I fought it.

I could sleep when I was dead, which was a possibility as long as Apollo was carrying around whatever messed up vendetta he had that no one else understood.

I took a deep breath and listened to the thumping of his heart.

It hurt to think that the same heart that I was listening to, the one that rested just inches away from my face, was breaking.

It was broken, obviously, and Apollo felt like he had to hold it all in. Like he had to keep it all together.

And for me, that hurt more.

I wanted him to know that he could talk to me about anything, and under any other circumstance, he would. He wasn't shy about cussing me out or arguing with me, so why was he about talking about his past?

It hurt even more that I had bits and pieces of it, but none of them were from him.

I had to learn second-hand information from other people, and I didn't know if it was because he didn't know how to talk about it or if he didn't feel like I deserved to know.

Either way, I was determined to find out.

I understood what it felt like to feel alone, not knowing if you had anyone to trust. I also knew what it felt like to find out the one person you thought you could, stabbed you in the back.

Neither feeling was pleasant.

And I swore that I didn't want anyone I cared about to feel them.

So I did something bold- something that I couldn't quite tell if it was smart or idiotic.

I said her name.

"I know about Daya." The words tumbled out of my mouth before I had time to stop them, but if I was honest, I wasn't sure if I would have if I were given a chance.

They tumbled out so fast that they were almost a blurred mess, and the long silence that came afterward almost had me convinced that he hadn't even understood what I said.

But hearts are fickle creatures, and his told on him in an instant.

What was once a slow and monotonous beat turned into a fast-paced thrum of thudding inside his chest, and I knew.

Just by the sound of his heart, I knew I fucked up.

And when it came to Apollo, there was no telling how bad it truly was until I found myself in the eye of the storm.

He ripped himself out from underneath me, sending my body colliding back down to the mattress, and in an instant, he was on his feet, standing beside the bed, looming over me.

His hands were balled into fists at his sides, and there was a look in his eye that I'd never seen before. A crazed one that almost scared me.

"Where did you hear that name?" He said, his words hot with anger.

I froze, not sure what to do to make it right.

"I- I just- I" I stuttered.

"Where!" He yelled, his tone bringing tears to my eyes.

I hated it.

"Adler!" I yelled back without thinking, but the shift of anger in his gaze told me that I had fucked up twice in a row.

It was like every time I opened my mouth, I made the situation worse.

"I'm going to kill him." He said through gritted teeth and rushed to the door.

Shit.

"Apollo, no!" I jumped out of bed, praying to the heavens that I would catch him before he made it out of the doorway, but I wasn't as lucky as I'd wished for.

"Apollo!" I stumbled out into the hallway behind him, but he was already out of reach.

His water whip was out of his pouch, and he didn't even flinch at the sound of my voice.

I knew in the pit of my stomach that he was gone. He was blinded by the anger that seeped into his soul. I didn't know what happened, but for him to storm out like that, it had to be worse than I could ever imagine.

"Apollo!" I yelled down the hall again as he turned a corner and disappeared.

I was about to follow him when I noticed a group of girls snickering down the hall.

I cocked my head to the side, wondering what they could have possibly found so funny about his murderous intent, until I realized that, by the grace of God, I had fucked up a third time in a matter of minutes.

I was completely naked.

I threw my arms around my body in an attempt to shield whatever sliver of decency that I had left, but at that point, you would have needed a microscope to see it.

I bolted back into the room at lightning speed and rushed to pull my clothes on while my heart raced wildly in my chest.

Every second that it took me to get myself together, I knew Apollo was another second closer to probably ending Adler's life.

I didn't completely understand why he was so angry that I knew about Daya. He was usually an angry person, but the anger that washed over his face the second he heard her name was on a different level.

I couldn't help but think that there was more to the story than Adler, I or anyone else could have possibly known.

Aside from Apollo, of course.

I pulled up my zipper hastily and rushed out of the room, the girls still standing in the same place that they had been.

I froze for a moment when they saw me, my cheeks sizzling a light shade of pink, but I pulled myself out of it quickly.

What the hell was I doing, embarrassed because someone saw me naked when I was a freaking eden who could control all of the elements.

After everything that I had survived, someone seeing me naked should have been the least of my worries, especially when the clock was ticking on Adler's existence.

"I hope you got a good show." I half-laughed before I bolted down the hall in the direction that Apollo had stormed off in.

My mind was racing a million miles a second as I rushed through the dimly lit, stone hallway. As I ran through, there were people scattered about celebrating. They stood in groups throughout the castle, drinking red wine out of chalices and taking turns saying cheers for the King that had returned.

It was crazy how much they adored him, especially compared to how unenthused he had seemed when he was discovered.

Especially how hard he had fought to stay hidden when the kingdom woke up again.

Something was going on, a story behind it, one that I was sure I would need to get to the bottom of too.

I groaned as I pushed past the happy faces.

It seemed like that was happening more and more, mysteries uncovering themselves and me being the one left to untangle them.

But I had a feeling that it was only the beginning.

I didn't have the slightest clue where Apollo had gone, but I hoped if I kept rushing through the halls I'd eventually run into him.

But when the entire building started to shake I knew that I was too late.

It started.

All I could do was hope that Adler was strong enough to hold him back until I got there for backup.

Chapter Seven

By the time I burst into the corridor near the front entrance, the shit show had already started.

There were huge sections of the stone floor that Adler had clearly used his power to raise and use as shields because I had to weave between them.

One of the large wooden doors hung off its hinges, and there were obvious cuts in its surface from Apollo's water whip. I slowly made my way through, running my fingertips over the gouges as I walked by.

If it could make such a clean slice in something as solid as the sturdy wood, I didn't dare even think about what it could do to a person.

A crash sounded from outside the castle that was so loud I could feel the vibrations in my feet.

The second I realized that it was coming from the courtyard that we had entered through, I rushed outside, saw what was going on, and skidded to a halt with my jaw unhinged.

"Holy shit." I mumbled.

There was a flash of light beside me, and Silas appeared. He was wearing new clothes, fine silvers, and golds that made up a suit with many buttons on the front, and a golden crown rested atop his purple tresses of hair. His hands were shoved into the pockets of his pants casually.

"I know." He huffed. "They've gone completely mad."

His words said one thing, but the way his lips curled at the corners said another. There was a rough edge about Silas, a quiet part of him that loved the chaos.

He was a little mad himself.

In front of us was a battle unlike any one that I had seen before.

All four of the guys stood in the courtyard, each of them wielding their element against the others.

Atlas stood in the middle of a small tornado that had him hovering a few feet off the ground. Adler stood surrounded by vines that lashed out like a whip every so often in all directions. Asher held two fireballs in his fists at his side, and Apollo had a wall of water that he pulled from a nearby fountain and maneuvered it through the air.

"Insane." I mumbled. "They're completely insane."

"Love does that to a man." Silas said calmly.

My attention snapped back to him, and a knowing smile crossed his lips.

It was almost like he knew something that I didn't.

I didn't doubt it. He was a mage of time, after all. He said he'd gone back and tried to take out a fire mage, which meant that he had moved through time before. I wouldn't have doubted that he knew all of the answers that we were searching for, but it was against some weird time mage rule not to tell.

That would be my luck.

I turned my head back to the battle in front of me and fought my urge to rush straight in the middle.

I was still weak from everything that happened, on top of being exhausted and sleep-deprived. I didn't know if I had enough energy to take on Apollo, let alone all the others.

I took a few steps forward, just enough to rush down the few steps and bring myself closer to the action before I stopped to listen.

I was too far away before to notice that they were even speaking at all.

"You had no right to tell her about things that aren't your business!" Apollo screamed over the roar of Atlas' wind storm.

All eyes landed on Adler, and I noticed a wave of pure anger in his eyes that I'd never seen before.

Adler, the funny one. The one that could never take anything seriously and found ways to laugh even when the entire world quite literally fell apart around us. There he was, his gaze filled with an anger that burned hotter than the flames that Asher held at his side.

Something about what Apollo said stung him to the core, and I hated that I didn't know what it was. I didn't know what set him off like that, but I could tell that there wasn't any going back.

He let out an angry scream and threw his hands forward, the vines at his sides, shooting forward at his command in Apollo's direction.

They darted through the air so fast that they looked like nothing more than green blurs, and asher used his water whip to slice through the air.

Pieces of the vines dropped to the ground and the ones that were cut immediately shriveled up and landed on the ground in brown, dead, heaps.

Apollo grinned, his satisfaction impossible to hide.

That's what made it so painful to watch the last remaining vines stealthily creep across the cobblestone, wrap around his ankles, and flipped him upside down, suspending him in the air.

He was about to use his whip again when the vines wrapped around him and pressed his arms into his sides solidly.

Apollo wriggled and writhed, but as hard as he tried, he couldn't get his arms free, and I realized that without them, he couldn't lift a single droplet of water.

He channeled his power through his hands. Without them, he was just a ball of anger, nothing more.

"Let me go!" Apollo screamed."

Adler walked to him slowly and stopped a few feet away from

him. He was sure to be close enough for him to see the look in his eyes, but far enough to make sure he was still safe.

Then words spiraled from his mouth that I didn't see coming.

"You're not the only one who loved her." A heartbreak showed in his eyes that made mine ache too. "You're not the only one that knew her in ways no one else did."

The words shocked even Apollo, who suddenly stopped wiggling and pulled his brows together.

"Wait what?"

"We were in love, too, okay? You're not the only one who lost her when she died."

My mind was spinning.

At first, I thought he was lying, but the pain in his eyes and the way his voice quivered when he said it made it obvious that he was telling the truth.

How the hell had I missed that?

Daya was sleeping with them both?

A silence fell over the courtyard. By then, a group of onlookers had gathered behind me from inside the castle, and when I glanced over my shoulder, I noticed that there was a face in every window that faced us.

These people lived in the stone ages, but they were nosy as hell.

The wind slowly died down, and Atlas lowered himself to the ground.

"You guys too?" He said with pain in his eyes.

Adler and Apollo's heads turned so fast that I was sure they gave themselves whiplash.

"What the hell?" Asher yelled, and the fireballs in his hands grew bigger. "You all slept with my sister?"

His voice was an angry growl that sounded a lot more like the asher that I knew.

"And she's dead?" There was a twinge of pain embedded in the growl, and his hair erupted into wild flames too that danced on top of his head.

All three of the guys managed to look a combination of confused and afraid at the same time.

"What the hell? You knew that." Apollo yelled. "You're the one that killed her."

For a split second, I swore that. Isaw the flames die down like the oxygen was being sucked out of the atmosphere, and they were suffering. Still, I realized that sadness suffocated people like lack of oxygen suffocated flames.

And Asher couldn't breathe.

It only lasted a second before the denial visibly settled into his face.

He was completely broken one second, and the next, he went back to his normal shade of anger.

"You're lying." He muttered so quietly that I almost wasn't able to hear it.

There was a pause where no one knew what to say until he repeated himself, this time with so much anger that his flames exploded in height.

"You're lying!" He screamed.

I definitely heard it that time.

The flames burned so wildly that the heat that radiated from them was insane.

I was a good distance away, and I could still feel their warmth against my skin.

They were hot enough that Adler's vines shriveled up and fell to pieces, nearly dropping Apollo on his head.

He would have broken his neck and probably died if it wasn't for Atlas catching him on a gust of wind and softening the blow.

Asher took a step toward the guys, and they sprung into action. Apollo grabbed the water from the fountain once again and placed a wall between Asher and the three.

That only bought them a few seconds to scramble for a plan before Asher walked straight through it, the water evaporating around his body as he did.

I didn't see Apollo afraid often, but it made my stomach ache to the core when I did.

Apollo wasn't afraid of anything, ever. He wasn't even afraid of Asher back in our world, or whoever the hell it was.

There was something different about the anger that he had, something that set him apart from the Asher that loved to burn and destroy.

The other Asher's anger was stale. His hatred was rooted in his belief that the fire mages should rule. He believed it, but it didn't even come close to the anger and the pain that came from finding out that his sister was dead. It didn't compare to the pain that came from a broken heart.

Adler put up a wall of rock right behind the wall of water, and as Asher got closer, he extended it into a circle that entrapped Asher, and finally, the rock stretched over the stop sealing him inside.

"He's trying to smother the flames." Silas appeared beside me. "Smart move."

I sunk my teeth into my bottom lip nervously.

It was a smart move, but would it be enough to stop him?

And would it kill him?

No oxygen meant no flames, but it could also mean no more Asher. It was something that I had dreamed about ever since he had made my life a living hell- well, more of a hell than usual.

So why did the thought make my stomach hurt more? I couldn't have possibly found myself siding with a homicidal maniac, could I?

There was something different about him. I felt it, like a small twinge in the middle of my chest, when he'd first stumbled out of the doorway. And I felt it more and more as time went on.

The queasy feeling that I normally got around him, the one that told me to run the other way because pure evil emanated off of him, was gone.

All that was left was an odd feeling.

And it was there now.

It took everything inside of me not to run straight into the chaos and beg Adler to set him free, not to kill him, because his pain was real. There was no way he could fake it. It was the same pain that I felt for most of my life.

I gnawed on the inside of my cheek until it was raw.

And just when I was about to do it, a smoldering rose from the enclosure. A black spot slowly started to form on the pale gray surface like something was seeping through from the other side, and finally, there was a crash as Asher burst through the scorched rock like it was nothing.

I was far away, but I could tell he was crying, small flaming droplets running from his eyes.

In that instant I knew, Asher didn't kill his sister.

And I had to stop them before they killed each other and I didn't have a chance to tell them that.

Adler, Apollo, and Asher all readied themselves for a fight. Adler with his vines, Apollo with what little water he could scrounge up, and Atlas with a whipping tornado, and they all rushed each other.

I couldn't let it happen.

I refused to let them destroy themselves.

They weren't getting rid of me that easily.

I rushed in the middle of all of them as they charged forward from all sides, all toward me.

A strange, bubbly feeling rose in my chest, and I felt like I might explode before it radiated out of me in strange rainbow-colored waves. The waves washed over everyone, and they froze, all the way down to the flames and the droplets of water.

That's when my knees buckled underneath me, and everything

went black.

Chapter Eight

"Open your eyes, love." Silas's voice floated to me through the warm embrace of the darkness that entrapped me.

I could hear it echoing off the walls inside my mind, but part of me didn't care. It was the same part of me that was exhausted, sleep-deprived, and just wanted a break.

After finding out that the fate of the entire world quite literally rested on my shoulders, that I could control five elements instead of four, and that three of the people that I was possibly in love with all were in love with the same girl at one point in time, could you blame me?

"Come on, you beautiful, stubborn woman. I know you can hear me," Silas said, trying to coax me from my place once again.

But I was done, sick of having to put everyone first. I wanted to sleep, and I didn't care if the entire world crumbled around me as I did. I was no use to anyone if I was exhausted.

So back into the darkness, I sank, and I let Silas's voice fade away as I did.

***

I rolled over, the feel of satin sheets gliding against every inch of my exposed skin.

I rubbed at my eyes, a warm, rested feeling settling into my bones.

For once, I woke up feeling completely rested.

I rubbed at my eyes with a balled fist and stretched, a yawn escaping my lips.

"Sleeping beauty rises." Silas's voice came from across the room.

I opened my eyes to see him resting in a grand chair wrapped in shimmering golden fabric. He sat slouched, with his crown sitting crooked on top of his purple hair. His intricate jacket that I had admired earlier was unbuttoned and hung open, exposing his chiseled chest. He looked as relaxed as I felt, which was very.

"Did you sleep well, my love?" He raised a brow as the words tumbled out of his mouth in a sultry drawl.

There was something about the way that he said them that made me tingle in all the right places, and his accent wasn't even the most attractive thing about him.

"I did, actually." I smirked.

"You didn't hear me trying to summon you?"

"Oh, I did. I just didn't give a shit." The smile grew on my face.

It was a small gesture of defiance, and maybe one of the first times in my life that I put what I needed over what everyone else did. It wasn't big or life-changing, but it felt like it to me, and that was all that mattered.

I glanced down and realized that I was completely naked, covered in nothing but a satin sheet.

My eyes widened, and I scrambled backward, clinging to the sheet until my back pressed against the back of the headboard.

"Where the hell are my clothes?"

"Oh, do calm down love, it's nothing I haven't seen before, remember?" He winked before he made his way to the large armoire across the room and rummaged through it. "If you had woken up when I asked, maybe we would have been able to save your clothes, but alas, a queen needs her beauty sleep."

I tried to wrap my head around what the hell was going on. I really didn't even know what had happened.

"You basically exploded." Silas read the look on my face. "You should have seen it. It was magnificent, really, like a beautiful bomb detonating down there. All of the elements spilled out of you at once, fire, water, earth, air, *and* time. The first four destroyed your outfit, but don't worry. You froze time, so no one had time to see you in the nude."

"Wait. What?"

For a split second, I forgot I was naked and rushed to the

window. Whatever room we were in, it overlooked the courtyard, and sure enough, I got a glimpse of everyone, frozen still.

Even the water that Apollo was trying to raise hung still in the air.

"I did that? But how?" I asked, turning to Silas, who was trying as hard as he could to ignore the fact that I was completely naked.

"I don't know the answer to that. Something like that is advanced. So advanced, in fact, that it normally takes five time mages to complete at once. Yet you did it alone, without even trying."

There was a look of wonder in Silas's eyes. He was impressed, and I couldn't stop it from going straight to my ego.

I blushed before I realized that it wasn't an accomplishment.

It was a mistake.

"Wait, how far does it go?"

"At least throughout my entire realm. It's impossible to know if it reached your realm, too, unless we travel to it."

I thought for a second, letting his words sink in. This wasn't what I'd wanted. I needed to go down there, unfreeze the guys, and figure out what the hell was going on, with Asher, and Daya, and whoever the fuck was out there burning the castes to the ground.

"Okay, well, undo it." I shrugged.

Silas burst into laughter, his eyes closing tightly as he did.

I crossed my arms tightly, no idea what he thought was so funny, but I let him have his time and laugh it out.

Partly because he was super cute when he laughed, but that was beside the point.

"Are you done enough to tell me what the hell is so funny?" I growled.

"I just told you that it would take five of me to recreate your curse, and you want me to undo it alone? Have you lost your mind?" His white teeth glistened in the sunlight that spilled in through the window.

"Maybe." I pouted.

"I'm afraid that it will take far more than you and I to undo it, especially if you don't know what you did to create it in the first place. Think of it like baking a cake without a recipe. You have an idea of what you did to make it, but you can never recreate it perfectly because of that same reason."

Shit.

I groaned and slinked back to the bed, pulling the satin sheets back over my body to cover myself.

"Okay, so you're useless." I groaned. "But does that mean you can't find me any clothes either?" I raised a brow in his direction, my eyes grazing across the bare part of his chest that his open jacket revealed before ripping my eyes from it once again and forcing myself to focus.

I was in a shitty situation, and the only thing I could think of was Silas jumping my bones?

I'd come a long way from the old Eden. It was almost funny.

Almost.

Silas could feel it too. He eyed me up and down slowly. He wasn't even trying to be discreet about it. He wanted me to know he was thinking about all types of dirty things about me.

And the worst part was I liked it.

My butterflies danced in my stomach, and my clit tingled, but I forced myself to stay focused.

I had to figure out what the hell was going on, and the answers were more than likely not in Silas's pants- no matter how badly I wanted them to be.

I knew that it would take nothing short of a miracle to undo the hastily made action with my luck.

Was there a world record for how many times that I could fuck up in a single day? Because if there was, I was sure that I was going to break it.

"Your wish is my command." He said with a smooth and devilish smirk.

The way he said it made me want to blurt out all the dirty wishes that were rattling around inside my head, but I fought the urge.

I made a promise to myself in that moment that I was done fucking up. I was ready to be serious and get to the bottom of the chaos that had imploded because I was ready for it all to be over with. Not just in this realm, but in the next one too.

While Silas sifted through the clothes that hung in the armoire, I found my thoughts drifting to what life would be like back home when all of this was over.

I wondered what would happen to the guys. They were technically awakened just to teach me and restore balance.

When that happened, would they go back to the eternal slumber that I found them in?

My heart broke a little bit at the thought.

As much as I didn't want to and tried my best to avoid it, I was attached to them.

Every one of them.

And when all of this was said and done, I wouldn't have Jade anymore, I didn't have the house that we shared, and I didn't have a single friend to my name- except them.

They were more family than anyone I'd met in my life- hell, they felt more like family than my own mother.

My eyes started to water at the thought of losing them, and my fists clenched at my side.

That was it.

I made my mind up.

I didn't care about the laws of physics, or nature, or time. I didn't care if God himself descended from heaven and said that it was time for the guys to go back to their slumber- I wasn't going to let it happen.

Everything that happened over the last few weeks only taught me one thing- I get to decide how my story turns out. Sure, I was born an eden and had to live a crappy existence for most of my life, but the second I took the reins, I realized that I held a power that was stronger than anyone else's.

That was who I was.

And who I was wasn't about to let something as fickle as *fate* control who I was allowed to be with. No one was going to get in the way of that, especially not *Daya*.

I knew she was dead, and the guys loved her, and it was sad, but I couldn't help but feel a sick feeling in the pit of my stomach every time I heard her name. It was the same feeling I got whenever I saw Asher- well, the *bad* Asher.

I didn't need to know her to know that she wasn't the greatest person, the fact that the guys were all sleeping with her and didn't even know it was the first sign.

Sure I slept with them all too, but I made it clear from the start that I belonged to no one, and they all had a non-verbal agreement to share me.

It was different. It was consensual—a deal.

I couldn't say that much for whatever she had going on.

"Here you are, my lady." Silas turned and held up a large puffy dress and a corset with a smile.

I rolled my eyes. "Try again."

He chuckled and rummaged inside the abyss that was the armoire again and pulled out a different but equally puffy dress and raised a brow.

"No." I groaned and shoved past him to get to the armoire.

"I guess if a lady wants anything done right, she must do it herself, huh?" Silas said from behind me.

I didn't need to see his eyes to know that they were wandering in all the places they didn't belong. An icy feeling traced the curve of my hips. I could practically feel his gaze, and the way it made me tingle was infuriating.

I had shit to do, people to see, a world to save.

And still my pussy was screaming for attention. My clit was demanding to be heard.

And who was I to quiet the voices of women?

I spun around with fire in my eyes and found him lying on the bed, completely naked, his cock standing tall and hard.

"Well, it took you long enough."

Chapter Nine

I took a step toward Silas, his naked body lounging in all its glory, when a bright flash of light strobed in front of me, and he appeared.

He glanced down at me, his eyes glistening, and I felt the warm touch of his finger brushing against my cheekbone as he cradled my face in his hand.

I closed my eyes and leaned into the arousal that bubbled up inside of me.

The world was yet again falling apart, but when I was with one of the guys it felt like it paused-no pun intended. Each of them had their way of making time slow and my heart race.

"You're so beautiful." He said, his voice low.

He leaned in closer and closed in the space between us. His dick brushed against my thigh, and a shiver ran up my spine.

"And I can't wait to ravage every inch of your beautiful body and claim it as mine."

He grabbed either side of my arms, and in a split second, another bright flash of light erupted. There was a cold rush of air that swept across my bare body, and goosebumps spread up my arms.

The next thing I knew, we appeared on the bed. It slightly bounced beneath us, and I found myself on top of Silas, his body straddled between the weight of my thighs.

I smirked.

He loved his parlor tricks, but little did he know I had a few of my own.

I closed my eyes and channeled my air powers, letting them slowly creep down both of my arms before I summoned a small gust of wind to rise underneath Silas.

At the same time, I leveraged my weight and rolled over, using the wind to fling him on top of me, positioning him right where I wanted him to be, planted between my legs.

A surprised look spread across his face, followed by an impressed smirk.

"Impressive." He smirked.

"A queen is always in charge." I feigned his accent, and all it did was make his smile grow bigger.

I opened my legs wide and summoned another gust of wind

behind him that pushed his head down between my legs, his lips pressed against my pussy lips.

"Bon-appetit my King." I winked, and it did something sinful to him.

It was like it moved away from being impressed and took a dive into unlocking a ravenous lust inside him.

For a moment, there was a look in his eye, like one that I'd seen in all the guys at one point in time.

I didn't know how to describe it. It wasn't a spark because that had already happened when we first met. It was more like a knowing look, like a threshold that we all had to cross—the moment when we realize that what we shared was more than just lust-filled hookups.

It was the moment that we accepted that we were meant to be.

I had no idea how the universe had fucked up and mystically assigned me more than one destined partner, but then again, the universe kind of fucked up when it created someone who could control more than one element too, so it was fitting.

For once, it was a fuck up that I could get behind.

My legs were bent at the knee, and my flower was spread wide open, my petals his to devour. He slid his arms underneath both of my thighs and locked his arms on the outside, pulling my thighs to his ears like earmuffs.

A moan slipped from my lips as I felt his tongue part the dripping wet lips of my pussy, and he devoured my sweet taste.

The tip of his tongue danced delicately on the tip of my clit, like a ballerina, gentle but powerful all at the same time.

I didn't quite understand how he did it or how those two things could even go together, but I didn't care because the pleasure that washed over my body in waves melted all of my skepticism away.

I wouldn't have cared if we started levitating like we were possessed. As long as he kept eating me out, he could do anything he wanted to me.

He released my thighs from his iron grasp and finally came up for air, his chin dripping wet.

I thought it was one of the sexiest things I'd ever seen, my juices running down his lips, but then he used a single finger to wipe it off and seductively slid it between his lips to suck it clean, and my soul almost left my body, with his dark purple eyes locked onto mine.

That man did wicked things to me with nothing more than a look.

I wanted him to violate me in every way that he knew how.

I would have gladly let him.

He slid both of his hands underneath my ass, sure not to break our deadlocked eye contact, and lifted my bottom half off the bed. He managed to wiggle my legs onto his shoulders, and he hoisted my pussy higher in the air while my top half stayed anchored to the bed.

"That's much better. The lighting is much brighter up here." He smirked. "I like to play with my food while I eat it."

With that, he pulled my pussy to his lips, dragging me a few inches lower on the bed. My eyes nearly rolled to the back of my head, and my body tensed up at the pleasure.

I didn't think that it could have possibly gotten better, but somehow it did.

"You see, Love, everything in the universe- including space and time- is all about the angle." He smirked before tilting me even higher. "You change the angle, and you change the entire human experience."

He flicked my clit with his tongue, and I tangled my fingers in the smooth bed sheets, trying to anchor myself to something before this man robbed me of my soul and sent me spiraling into oblivion.

"Say my name." He panted his warm breath lapping against my clit like waves against an ocean shore. "I want to hear you moan for me."

The way he sounded when he spoke under his breath made me tingle, and his name tumbled out of my mouth.

"Silas." I moaned.

"Again." He commanded.

"Silas." I moaned again while his tongue massaged me.

"Louder."

"Silas!" I screamed out in pleasure.

I could feel him smiling as he ate me out. He liked to see me squirm, but even more so he liked to know that he was the one making me do it.

I was so close to the cusp, only seconds away from clamping my thighs around his face and coming all over that devilishly handsome mouth of his when he pulled away and set me back down on the bed.

My eyes shot down in his direction, my mouth hanging wide.

"What the hell! I was almost there! What did you do that for?" I groaned.

Silas crawled on top of me slowly, like an animal sizing up its prey, and a hungry look still lingered in his eyes.

He leaned in and kissed me slowly, with every ounce of passion in his body. I could still taste myself on the tip of his tongue, and I think that was what he wanted. To give me a little glimpse of the ecstasy that he was devouring.

The savory taste that had him hooked from the first second it touched his tongue, that now danced inside my mouth with mine.

He pulled away and looked into my eyes. "I know that love. But I'd rather feel you cum clamped around my dick instead."

He grabbed me and rolled over, flipping me on top of him like I'd done to him.

I smirked.

He was slick, and he knew how to use that gorgeous mouth of his, but I had picked up a few things over the last few times, and I was ready to show him that my mouth could feel just as good as his. I planted a kiss on his lips, then worked my way to his sharp jawline, down his neck, eventually leaving a trail of sultry kisses.

I loved that the lower I got, the more I could feel him breathe in sharply at the feel of my lips pressed against his bare skin.

The way he shivered beneath my touch boosted the sexual goddess inside of me. She fed off of it.

I made my way to his belly button, and from there I drug my lips all the way down to his cock before planting a single kiss right on the time.

I looked up at him with a steel gaze and licked the salty taste of his precum from my lips, not letting my eyes waver for a single second.

I wanted to know he was watching me as I enjoyed every drop of him. And I wanted him to look me in the eyes as he watched his cock slide to the back of my throat.

I put the head of his dick between my lips and slowly took every inch of him into my mouth, staring intently into the beautiful purple pools.

My eyes watered as his cock made it to the very back, and tears ran down my cheeks but all that did was send an extra rush of blood to his dick, making it harder inside my mouth. I squeezed the base of his cock and moved my hand and my head in tandem, making sure to squeeze out every drop of delicious juice it was willing to give me.

A sexy mixture of a growl-like moan tumbled out of his mouth and sent a rush of adrenaline through me.

I pulled his cock out of my mouth and jacked him off, my eyes glued to his.

"Say my name." I demanded just like he had.

It caught him off guard and turned him on all at the same time, I could tell by the signature smirk that crept across his face.

"Eden." He said quietly.

"What was that? I couldn't hear you."

"Eden." The sound of him moaning my name alone was almost

enough to push me over the edge.

"Again. Who's your queen?" I smirked.

"Eden!" He moaned, and his dick quivered in my hand.

There was a flash of light and he teleported behind me, leaving my fist suddenly empty.

He pushed me forward on my hands and knees and without a single warning slid his cock inside of my pussy, all the way to the back, filling me completely.

"You're not my Queen until I fill you." He moaned. "It's ceremony."

I didn't quite understand what he was saying, but the way he moaned the word Queen rubbed me in all the right places and the way he fucked me from behind made my head spin.

"Say it again."

Silas grabbed me by my shoulders, and pulled me up so my back was straighter while he rammed his cock into me.

"Queen." He moaned in my ear.

That was it.

That was what pushed me over the edge.

I moaned loudly as my body clamped down, massaging his cock even harder, sending him into overload too. We came at the same time and Silas dumped his warm load inside of me.

I loved the feeling. I couldn't stop the smile that spread across my face and I crawled to the opposite side of the bed to pant in peace.

Silas moved to take the place beside me, his eyes full of wonder.

"So, would you want to be?" He turned to look at me.

I was a sweaty mess but the truth was I was too exhausted to care.

"Would I want to what?" I raised a brow.

"Be Queen, here with me of course." Silas said catching me off guard. "It's the law of the country that the person that the King gives his virginity to will become the Queen."

Chapter Ten

"Wh-What?" I stammered like an idiot, even though he had already clearly repeated himself.

My heart pounded in my chest, and a wave of nervous heat washed over my body.

I racked my brain trying to figure out when it had gone from me trying to unhealthily process my emotions with sex, to me becoming the Queen of an entire realm, to a man that I barely knew.

And virginity?

What virginity?

That man railed me like a porn star.

I got up from my place on the bed and scrambled for my clothes, blubbering like an idiot the entire time.

If I was being honest, I had no idea what I was even saying. It was apparent that I was avoiding the question, and Silas was far from stupid.

But instead of getting hot-headed and angry like Apollo would have, his face remained calm and collected.

He lounged in the bed, with his hand tucked behind his head. His eyes trailed every movement I made but in a curiously nonchalant kind of way.

I hated that I could feel my cheeks burning red.

Why the hell was I so flustered? I was sure there were a million girls out there that would have thrown themselves at Silas purely because of his chiseled abs and sharp jaw. That's not even factoring in his charm and the accent.

But why did someone trying to commit to me make my skin want to crawl? Why did the thought of actually having something that would be mine, and mine alone make me feel like the earth beneath my feet was quaking?

Was I that traumatized?

"Well- I- You see-" I stammered.

"Don't have an aneurysm, love." Silas held up a hand, his accent calm and collected. "It wasn't a proposal. It was a question."

There was a flash of light, and in an instant, he stood in front of me. The space between our two bodies was so narrow that I could feel the heat radiating off of his chest. There was an electricity that bounced around in the room between us, one so potent that it made the air feel light.

There was something there, something magical about us together. There was no denying that. But the same was true about all the other guys. Each of them held a piece of my heart and knew how to keep every other part of me, too, in ways that made me not want to let any of them go.

Even Asher, as much as I hated that it was true, there was no denying the spark that we'd shared.

Silas brought his hand up to my cheek and caressed it with a single finger before letting his hand drop beneath my chin and guiding my eyes up to meet his.

"A question that I'd love for you to consider." He said, his voice soft.

He tugged at my chin, pulling my lips to his in the most aggressively gentle way known to man, and I tingled in all the right places.

The kiss was slow and long, with the tiniest bit of sweetness at the edges that made the butterflies in the pit of my stomach dance for joy.

I felt like my breath was being sucked from my lungs, pulled from my body by the chemistry that we shared, and when it was over, I desperately wanted it to happen again.

But it couldn't.

It would be way too easy for me to forget myself in this pocket of time.

With everything on pause, there was too much of a chance for me to let time get away from me.

To stay there forever, living between the sheets of the king's chambers, with a gorgeous purple hunk at my side.

"Tell me, how the hell do we break this thing for good?" I changed the subject and zipped up the trousers that Silas had scrounged up from the wardrobe for me.

I turned away from Silas awkwardly as he got dressed and gazed out the window, pretending to be particularly entranced by the frozen beauty of his realm.

I couldn't help but peek over my shoulder a few times, though, to get a good look at the chiseled perfection behind me.

"Well, that is the question now," Silas said, perplexed. "Because the more I think about it, the less it makes sense."

"The less I think about it, the less it makes sense." I mumbled.

There wasn't a single thing about anything going on that followed any notion of common sense. That was the most frustrating part.

I gazed back out at the window, my eyes gazing across the morning sky. There were a few birds suspended in the air as if they were hanging from an invisible thread. A flash of light erupted over my shoulder, and I felt Silas's presence behind me. His hands slid over my hips and rested in front of me, lingering just above my waistline, leaving a trail of tingles behind them.

"Look forward." He leaned and whispered in my ear, his warm breath soothing. "Tell me what you see."

"Your frozen kingdom." I said flatly.

I didn't know what he was getting at, but even with a face as gorgeous as his, it was getting a little frustrating how every word that left his lips sounded like a riddle. Silas spoke in puzzles and codes, a language all his own. The rest of us were left to try to decipher what it was, he meant.

But in a way, that was part of his mystery, the reason I was roped in. I couldn't deny it.

"Look further." He whispered, oddly sensually, his tone waking every part of my body.

I squinted my eyes, and there was a flash of light, this time ripping Silas from my side.

His kingdom was immense and stretched for most of the span of my sight, but after all the houses, buildings, and farms ended, there was something else—a sea of tan and beige.

Silas appeared again, beside me, this time with a looking glass that glistened in the sunlight. It was made of gold and had the most intricate embellishing that I'd ever seen. Symbols were etched into it in swirls, and x's that wrapped around its rounded edges perfectly. It was an intriguing thing to look at, and the second he handed it to me, I couldn't help but brush my fingertips across the rough grooves of each symbol.

Something about it called to me. It looked oddly familiar, even though I was more than positive that I'd never seen anything like it in my entire life.

"Look again."

I brought the glass up to my eye and telescoped it out, feeling like a pirate gazing across the open seas, and suddenly everything was clear as day. My gaze stretched far beyond the outskirts of the kingdoms, even surpassing the outlying farms, and I realized the sea of beige was a desert, covered in sand.

"A desert."

"Yes, a desert." Silas said, his voice a chipper smile. "But what's past that?"

"I don't know. It doesn't go that far."

Silas laughed, and I couldn't tell what was smoother, the low, delicious tone of his voice or his laugh.

It rubbed me in ways that I'd never felt before, and I had to force myself to focus on the task at hand.

"It goes as far as you want it to. Try again."

I rolled my eyes. Did he think I was stupid? It couldn't be that complicated to operate a medieval piece of technology. It was as simple as bringing your eye to it and looking out. Right?

I pulled it away from my face and glared at him.

But all he did was smirk and nod.

"If you put as much energy as you are into having an attitude into making it work, it would work in an instant. You're cute, though."

I forced another groan and pulled the glass back to my eye before he could see the smile spread across my lips.

"And all I see is the desert."

"Then you're not trying hard enough."

I was about to snap back at him until his words rattled around in my head.

Maybe he was on to something.

Instead of throwing my energy into thinking of a sarcastic

response, I simply took a deep breath and concentrated. At first, nothing happened, but then the edges of my vision slowly started to blur, and the next thing I knew, the scope was zooming in further, all the way past the desert that stretched across a vast section of land beyond the kingdom. The scenery sped past, and I almost got dizzy at the rate it was zeroing in. I was about to fall back when it finally stopped, and the world didn't feel like it was spinning any more.

"Holy shit. It worked."

"What do you see?" Silas asked curiously.

He almost sounded surprised that it had worked.

In front of me was a vast ocean. I scrunched my nose at it. The water wasn't blue. It was a vibrant shade of pink. So vibrant that it almost didn't look real.

"I see an ocean, a pink one." My words came out more like a question than I had intended. "Wait a minute, and the waves are moving. Aren't they supposed to be frozen like everything else?"

I pulled the glass from my eye and looked at Silas before stumbling back a few steps from the drastic change in vision.

He leaped forward and caught me before I had an untimely encounter with the stone floor.

"Those are the seas of time. They don't stop for anything, even curses."

His arms were clasped tightly around my shoulders as he hoisted me back to my feet.

I turned the looking glass over in my hands, suddenly ashamed that I had thought of it as medieval technology.

It was probably more advanced than anything I'd ever laid a finger on back in my realm.

"What is this?"

"It's what we call the explorer's gaze. It's a mystical thing, enchanted by the lords of time, that is said to reveal the will of the universe."

An odd-sounding snort made its way out of me, and Silas's eyes snapped in my direction.

"I'm sorry." I stuttered, my cheeks warming once again. "It's just hard for me to believe that the universe has any sort of will." I shrugged. "And if it does, it has a whole lot of bad will for me and my life. We have a history of not seeing eye to eye. We go way back."

Silas rolled his eyes this time. It was odd to see a look of sarcasm in his eyes. "The universe knows what it's doing. And the glass points you to it."

"Oh yeah? What if I look this way?" I smirked and aimed it in the complete opposite direction, at a random stone wall in the castle.

I extended it and brought it to my eye, ready to prove Silas wrong, when something came over me and spun me backward until the glass pointed back out to the sea. I felt like a magnet being moved by an invisible force.

"What the hell?" I looked at Silas, shocked.

"Yeah, fate isn't something that you can necessarily outrun." He smirked, a look of satisfaction in his eyes.

"Oh yeah? Well, what does it show you?" I raised a brow and

shoved it in his direction.

He paused for a moment and thought about whether he should take it or not before sliding it from my grip.

I moved out of the way and stood in front of the wardrobe, thinking he would gaze out the window like I had, but instead, he copied me, pointing it in a random direction at a wall. He brought it to his eye, and in an instant he was spun around, and his gaze was fixed in a different direction, straight at me.

Chapter Eleven

The electricity hung in the air and I stood as frozen as everything else around me when the telescope landed on me. While my body was frozen, my mind and my heart were two different stories.

I didn't know what I thought was happening until that moment, with each of the guys. The sparks were there. I knew they were my destined mates, but for some reason, that took a back seat to all the immediate danger that always seemed to follow. I was too busy running for my life or trying to save it for my brain to process it fully.

But there, with the gaze of fate pointed in my direction, it finally hit me.

The universe was a sarcastic bitch, and five partners were all part of it. I had grown up thinking that I would be alone forever, and the universe had sent me not one but five partners just to complicate my life.

"We should go." I said the words so quickly that they all blended into one long slur.

"Go where?" Silas asked, calmly lowering the looking glass from his eye.

"I don't know. Wherever we need to fix this."

I was deflecting. I knew it, but even more so, Silas knew it.

He wasn't just a walking puzzle, he was a walking puzzle solver, and I was one that he already unraveled.

I didn't wait for his response before I spilled out into the hallway of the unfamiliar castle. I had no idea where I was going or even how to get there, but I put one foot in front of the other and didn't wait for him to catch up.

My mind was racing a million miles a minute, but the most disturbing thing had to be the way my stomach churned. It was a sick, bubbling feeling deep in my core, and I couldn't help but realize that it wasn't the fact that Silas was interested in me that made me uncomfortable or any of the other guys for that matter.

It was the fact that I didn't feel like I was deserving of it.

It was one of the most frustrating feelings in the world. Even after all the growing that I'd done, all the mastering of my powers, I was still my own biggest enemy.

I was the most powerful mage in the world; there was no doubt about it. No one else alive could do what I could do, and while I was a completely different person than I was before any of it started, there were still slivers of the old me that lingered inside. Parts of the Eden who felt abandoned her entire life slowly rose to the surface. The version of me that thought everyone who ever complimented her was lying to her face, the one who basically got walked all over for a living.

It was her that couldn't accept it. Any of it.

And that fucking sucked.

It wasn't like I didn't want five handsome men feigning over me. It wasn't like I didn't want to get to be the hero for once, I did.

I wanted to be the one who got to swoop in and show the world that it was wrong about me. The girl that they thought wasn't good enough for anything could slay dragons and save the day.

But it was that one small piece of the old me that held me back. The voice that told me I wasn't good enough, and I never would be.

It rose to the surface now and then to disrupt my peace and make me question my existence, and it was back at it again, this time with a vengeance.

If it had been Apollo or Atlas, or maybe even Adler, they would have rushed out after me.

They would have stormed the castle searching for me, hunt me down, and make me face my demons.

But Silas was different.

As I marched through the empty halls and made my way around the occasional frozen person, I kept expecting to hear his footsteps behind me or see his flash of bright light to talk some sense into me, but it never came.

Instead, I pranced through the halls on autopilot. I wasn't sure where I was going or why. I just wandered until something stopped me in my tracks.

I found myself back at the chamber that held the time clock.

The door to the room was slightly ajar, and there was a mystical shimmering light shining from inside that called to me the moment my eyes fell on it. It was like a beacon that roped me in and pulled me closer.

I had no idea where I was wandering until I saw it, and I knew I was going for it the entire time.

It was a shimmering mix of golden light that spilled out through the narrow crack in the door. In a land frozen, its beams still danced and swayed, and for a split second, I swore that I could hear voices coming from inside the room.

I took a step forward and nudged the door open with my foot, unleashing a bigger beam of the gorgeous light to spill out into the hallway.

My eyes widened at its beauty, and it pulled me in further.

"Eden." A whisper of a voice echoed off the walls when I stepped inside.

I glanced over both shoulders, spooked.

"Who's there?" I called out, my voice shaking slightly.

"Eden." The disembodied voice whispered again.

This time it was easy to tell that it wasn't coming from behind me or around me. It was coming from in front of me.

It was coming from the time clock that sat inside the glass chest.

I cocked my head to the side, curiously at it, and took a step further.

On autopilot, my hand reached out in front of me, and I pressed my hand up against the cold, smooth glass of the chest. The second my hand touched the glass, there was a bright flash of light, and the chest disappeared, leaving nothing but the time clock standing on an empty podium.

I blinked a few times, trying to wash my eyes of the light that nearly blinded me, before taking it all in.

The clock itself was mesmerizing, not to mention all the shimmering glitter that it held.

I couldn't help but stare at it.

If the things Silas had said about it were right, it wasn't just a clock at all. It was a tool, one that could be key to helping me end the fiery reign of Asher, or the wrong Asher, or whatever the hell we were calling the person who was wreaking havoc on everything that I'd ever known.

I thought about what he'd said about timelines and changes and how all it would take was a small change in the past to make a big one in the present.

I reached out and grabbed the clock from the podium, half expecting some booby trap to activate like an old Indiana Jones movie, but the room was silent.

I held the clock tightly, remembering that each glittering grain that filled it wasn't sand but a moment in time, or a reality like Silas had said. I wasn't sure how that worked or why, but I knew that wasn't the kind of thing you wanted to spill all over the floor.

I brought it up to eye level and inspected the contents.

All I could think about at that moment was what I would do if I ever mastered the element of time. If time and space didn't confine me, I knew where I would go, hands down.

A tear ran down my cheek as I thought about it. It pooled at my chin before falling from my face and landing in a single droplet on top of the time clock, triggering some sort of reaction. A bright warm light started to glow from inside, a soft yellow. I wiped at my cheek and cocked my head to the side just as a gush of warm air exploded from inside it, and the light consumed me completely like an orb.

Everything went white.

***

My vision didn't come back all at once. It slowly trickled in. The sounds were the first thing to hit me. The sounds of feet shuffling, somewhere far off, echoing down an empty hall.

As my vision slowly returned, I realized that I was back in the manor, more confused than I'd ever been.

Down the hall, I caught the back half of Johnathon scurrying around the corner.

I followed after him, with the time clock still in my hands. I didn't know what was going on, but the way that Johnathon was rushing made me think it was a big deal.

I trailed him closely until I realized he was going to the suite that I stayed in and slowed my pace.

He made his way inside and shut the door partly, leaving only a crack open.

A woman's voice floated out from inside, light and airy, but happy all the same.

It took me a few minutes to realize that she wasn't talking. She was singing a nursery rhyme, which seemed to confuse me even more.

My heart thudded in my chest, unsure if I should make a run for it or investigate, but it was no surprise that my curiosity got the best of me.

I took a few steps forward and, as quietly as I could, pressed my eye up against the crack and peered inside, my jaw-dropping at the same time.

Inside, sitting comfortably in bed, was my mother.

Well, a younger version of her anyway.

And cradled in her arms was a sleeping baby- me.

I held my breath as my head reeled. How was it possible? Where the hell was I?

Baby Eden stirred in my mother's arms, and I watched her caress my tiny cheek with a single finger, her eyes filled with nothing but love and adoration.

"Holy fuck." I whispered.

I couldn't stop the words from falling from my lips, and the second that they did, my mother's eyes snapped up from the child in her arms in the direction of the door.

"Johnathon." An alarming look spread across her face. "Did you hear that?"

"I'll check it out at once, madam." Johnathon said smoothly.

Shit.

I backed away from the door as quickly as I could in a panic.

I hadn't done anything wrong, and I most definitely didn't have a thing to hide about, but Silas's warning rang in my ears. The smallest change in the past could make a significant change in the present.

While I wasn't sure if this was a trip to the past or just a hallucination, I didn't want to take any chances of fucking up the present even more than it already was.

I backed away from the door and took entirely too long, trying to decide which way I should run down the hallway.

I panicked and headed further down the hall instead of tracing my steps back the way that I had come and managed to sprint around the corner just as I heard the door to the room open.

"Hello?" Johnathon's voice came from down the hallway. "Is anyone there?"

I peeked around the corner with only one eye and held my breath.

Johnathon wasn't stupid.

In fact, he was one of the smartest people I'd ever met, made of water or not.

So the weight I felt leave my shoulders when he decided to let it go and close the bedroom door was immense.

I breathe a sigh of relief. "That was a close one." I whispered to myself.

I spun around to make my way down the hall and crashed into someone, my body and the time clock spiraling to the ground.

"No!" I yelled a little too loudly at the horrific thought of the clock shattering.

But then a small tornado of win formed underneath it and cushioned it, making it hover just above the ground.

I looked at it in awe at the fact that I could have done that but didn't.

I gazed up to see who was responsible, and my eyes widened at my father towering over me, with a look just as shocked as mine on his face.

Chapter Twelve

My father's eyes darted from the clock, to me, back to the clock, and I could see the gears were turning behind his eyes.

He looked so young and so vibrant, just like the portrait that hung on the wall of the manor.

If it wasn't for that, I wouldn't have known it was him.

I held my finger up to my lips to shush him and got to my feet, praying with everything in me that I could make it out of this quickly. I had no idea how to use the clock, but I knew every second that I stayed was more time for the universe to mess up the present. Who knew what disastrous effects my being there had.

I knew I didn't want to find out. Especially when fate hadn't been kind to me in the past.

I reached for the clock but my father moved his gust a wind so the clock slid out of my reach.

I rolled my eyes and let my power flow through my arms.

It was getting easier and easier to do, almost like a second nature.

I created my own gust of wind, just like Atlas had shown me, and pulled the clock from his, carrying it to my hands.

"So you're an air mage." My father's voice cut through the quiet solace of the hallway and made me nervous.

The last thing I needed was for more people to see me. Even hearing me was too much of a risk.

"No I'm not here. You never saw me." I whispered, clutching the clock tightly, I slowly backed up, fully ready to make a run for it.

"Is that why you're holding half of the sands of time?" My father called out, his words stopping me in my tracks.

I spun around and glared at him.

It was off to be staring him in the face instead of gazing up at his portrait, and it was even weirder to think that he wasn't more than a few years older than me.

"How do you know what this is?" I said, my voice a loud whisper.

"The same way I know that you're not supposed to be here, are you?" He smiled. "Eden."

My jaw nearly hit the floor, but my lips couldn't help but curl at the edges.

My eyes started to water at the way he said my name, so soft and knowing. I was a newborn. I couldn't have been more than a few hours old in his world, but still he took one look at me, as an adult and he knew.

"How did you know?"

"You look like your mom." He took a step forward and reached out, tucking a lock of hair behind my ear in the sweetest way. "But I can see the Montgomery in you."

When I noticed the tears that danced in his eyes, it was too much for me to keep mine in too.

My dead father was standing in front of me, living and breathing. How many people were able to get that opportunity?

Warm streams ran down my face.

He took one look at the way I fell apart, and he knew.

He didn't have to say it and neither did I.

I could tell that he knew that I never got to know him.

"Walk with me." He waved me on to follow him.

"But what if someone sees me? It could ruin the timeline."

"Not necessarily. You see, maybe in your timeline this had already happened, you just didn't know it yet. Just because you hadn't gotten to the point where you traveled back, it didn't mean that you hadn't already." He said as we slowly made our way down the hall.

My head hurt just thinking about it.

The element of time was new to me, not including time travel. It all seemed like such a big and overwhelming subject, but the words fell from his lips like it was the easiest thing to understand.

He must have noticed the look on my face, because he elaborated.

"The easiest way I can explain it is that time isn't a straight line. It's not like a tightrope of events arranged all neat and tidy that we walk every day. It's like a loop, a sphere if you will, and everything circles back, everything is connected, even if it doesn't seem like it."

I looked up at him, and he laughed. "But I'm guessing by the look on your face that you didn't come here to ask me about that."

"Not exactly." I gnawed on my bottom lip.

"Then what?"

I thought in silence for a moment and he let me quietly trail him through the house, strategically avoiding all of the main rooms until we made it out the back door. The temple came into view, and even that looked different, fresher.

"I don't know why it brought me here." I looked down at the clock that I cradled in my hands. "I was having a hard time with everything, and it just did."

My father nodded. He was puzzled, but there was no denying that happy look in his eyes.

"I don't get to see you like this, do I?" He asked, his question catching me off guard. "I don't get to see you grow up."

I paused and. took a deep breath. Somehow even the air seemed lighter than back home at the manor. It must have had something to do with a lot less existential dread looming overhead.

It was a beautiful day, the sun was shining brightly and there was a slight breeze that balanced it out.

Cool. Calm. Perfect.

It was the day his daughter was born- I was born.

I didn't want to be the one to break the bad news to him.

It must have been written on my face, because he cleared his throat. "You're right, don't answer that."

I rubbed at the back of my neck with my freehand awkwardly.

"There must be a reason you're here. What do you need?"

He asked the question so casually, like I was just a normal adult child who stopped by to steal some food out of their fridge and mooch off their wifi, not like I was someone who had just appeared from the literal future.

"I don't know." I admitted. "There's a lot going on in-" I paused trying to figure out how to phrase it.

"The future." He finished.

I nodded. "Yes. There are some pretty big things happening, and I'm the only one who can stop them."

I looked up at him, expecting him to be amazed, or proud, or something, but instead he looked on blankly, waiting for more.

"And?"

"What do you mean and? Is that not enough?" I bugged my eyes out at him, and he laughed.

"You have your mom's attitude."

I rolled my eyes but couldn't help but smile. He seemed funny, the kind of dad that told it like it was, but in a way that you couldn't help but laugh, and it should have made me smile but instead I felt a familiar ache rise up in the pit of my stomach at the thought that he never got to share that side of himself with me.

He never got to share much with me really.

And that was what stung the most.

"Honey, we're edens. That's what our life is like all the time, trust me. There's always some threat, some simmering war between the elements that you need to put out, some person you need to put in their place."

I sighed.

Did that mean that my life was going to be like that forever?

Or would I be like him and have it cut short because of it?

He must have noticed my gaze faltering because he did something that I didn't expect.

He took a step forward, pulled me into his arms, and held me tightly.

At first it was awkward, but the longer it went on I could feel it melt away, with nothing left but a warm fuzzy feeling that I didn't get to feel as often as I would have liked- love.

He smelled like cologne and cheeseburgers, two of my favorite things, and I caught my eyes watering up again before I hugged him back.

"I just don't know if I can do it." I sobbed into his shoulder.

"Do what?" He pulled my head back to look at him.

"Be you." I sighed and wiped at my tears. "You're selfless. You just had a kid a few hours ago and now you're talking about how it's just part of your job to save the world and keep the peace all in the same breath. You're not stressed, you're not afraid, you're *you*. I don't know if I can be that."

He thought for a moment before nodding in understanding. He grabbed my hand and marched me back into the house where we had come. This time he had a blazing look of determination in his eyes that I hadn't seen in person before, but I recognized it. It was the same strong, determined gaze that they had depicted in his portrait.

This time he didn't even tiptoe. He didn't make an effort to hide from anyone, and I knew that it was because wherever we were going, and whatever he thought he had to do was more important than that in his eyes.

He pulled me through the hallways, past all the portraits, to a dead end hallway that I didn't remember ever seeing in my version of the manor. At the end of the hallway was a bookcase. He walked up to it and slid his fingertips across the spines of the books until he reached a certain one, tilted it, and took a step back.

We watched as the bookcase slid out to reveal a secret room.

"I shouldn't even be surprised. This place is filled with secrets." I smirked.

"You don't know the half of it." He said as he pulled me inside the room and the bookcase slid closed behind us.

"I have to be quick. You don't have much time left."

I opened my mouth to ask how he knew, until I realized that the time clock was blinking a faint shade of blue.

Then it clicked in my mind.

"You've mastered time too, haven't you?" I smirked.

"I was the first ever eden to." He said with a smile while he rummaged through a series of books arranged on a shelf against the wall.

The room was an office that held a desk, a single window, and a bunch of bookshelves.

"I'm not sure what exactly you're fighting, but you're right that it's probably best that I don't know the details. While time is more complex than just a straight line, you can never be too careful, especially if it's your first time time jumping, and it looks like you only have one of the clocks, which means half the power. But I want you to know two things." He finally found the book that he wanted and pulled it from the shelf.

It was a journal wrapped in dark leather and tied with a string to be held shut.

He looked at it longingly, like he wasn't ready to say goodbye to it just yet.

"What are the two things?"

"I love you. And you can do this." He smiled with tears in his eyes as my clock blinked faster. He rushed to me, folded the journal into my hand, and pulled me into one last hug. "You're an eden. You come from a bloodline so pure and so strong that the laws of nature had to bend for them. Don't forget that."

He took a step back and with tears rushing down his face he waved goodbye. There was a bright flash of light and the next thing I knew I was standing back in the room in Silas's castle, the time clock in one hand and the journal in the other.

Tears rushed down my cheeks but for the first time in a long time they weren't tears of sadness- they were tears of relief.

Chapter Thirteen

I stood in the room for a few minutes silently, letting myself feel all of the emotions that ran through my body.

It wasn't something that I was used to doing, but it was something that was necessary. I realized that I had been so focused on trying to push through everything that I wasn't giving myself enough time to feel everything, and that was a big reason as to why I was feeling so overwhelmed.

I may have been a magical badass, but I was a magical badass who was also human. I was my biggest critic, and it was time for that to stop.

By the time Silas found me my tears had dried and I was making my way out of the room with the time clock in hand.

"There you are. I was worried bloody sick about you."

"What, were you afraid someone was going to kidnap me? Everyone's frozen, remember?" I smiled with a thick layer of sarcasm on my face and Silas smirked too.

I could tell by the glint in his eye that he knew something about me was different. The second his eyes landed on the clock in my eyes they widened.

"I knew if anyone was going to be able to get it out of the case it was sealed in, it would be you."

"Of course. I am an eden, remember?" I raised my eyebrows proudly. "Now all we need to do is figure out what the hell is going on, what it has to do with the time clocks, and how I can fix it."

"So just another normal day for you." Silas smirked.

"Got that right." I smiled.

From there I led myself through the hallways, backtracking the steps that we had taken until we made it to the large corridor near the front entrance. I made it down the stairs and spotted a person standing near the doorway with a backpack on that would be perfect for the clock.

I whispered a redundant apology for boosting it as I slipped it off his shoulders and dropped the clock and the journal inside.

Silas opened the flap and added the looking glass too.

I made my way back into the courtyard and groaned at the group of angry men that stood frozen in it. They were just as I'd left them, angrily fighting, frozen with the elements that they had been hell-bent on using as weapons. They were the same and I knew it, but I, on the other hand, felt different.

I felt rejuvenated, like I had a new sense of purpose, and for the first time in a while I believed in myself.

I didn't know what was in the journal that my father had slipped into my hands, but I trusted that I would know what to do with it at the right time.

That was more than I could say for the guys.

"Would you like to hear my theory?" Silas asked as I stared at their frozen faces in frustration.

"Go for it."

"I don't think breaking the seal and releasing Asher broke the curse. I don't think it was ever over, but I think it was you who paused it."

"Paused?"

"It was a momentary air bubble in the water that is the curse, and in the moment that you saw Asher, I think it was your own emotions that were strong enough to hold it back, even just momentarily."

I thought about what he said, and it made sense- at least the part that I understood.

When I saw Asher stumble out of the doorway there was an explosion of confusion and anger and relief all rolled into one potent cocktail.

"When it comes to the element of time, it's not about brute strength to fuel your power, or your intelligence and wit, it's about the emotion that you can fuel through it. The best mages of time have mastered the element not because they were born with the talent, or they exercised it, but because their emotions behind wanting to master it were so potent and pure that the universe had no other choice but to grant them their hearts deepest desires.

I thought back to the sadness that I'd felt in the room, and a single tear that slid down my cheek and landed on the timeclock. It wasn't just filled with sadness, it was filled with despair, and defeat, and exhaustion. It was mixed with all the emotions that I hadn't let my body expel.

It was the definition of an emotional cocktail.

And it was the reason the clock took me back to the moment in time that I needed most.

I needed to meet my father, I needed to see my mother happy, and I needed to see them both lovestruck over having me. I needed to know that I wasn't an accident, or a fluke in the universe. I was wanted, and loved then by two people, and it was time for me to accept the fact that I was wanted and loved now by five.

"Okay." I nodded. "So what do I need to do to break the curse completely?"

"Well first things first, you need the other clock. The one you have in your hands controls all of the positive timelines, the happy things in life, the pleasant realities. In order to fully master time you need the one that holds the disasters too."

My stomach churned at the words.

It was always something. The universe always had to throw in some curveball. Some impending doom, or in this case, a time clock filled with it.

If he had told me this even a few minutes ago, it would have probably scared me away.

But I didn't even bat an eye, because the words that my father had told me still rattled around inside my head.

I was an eden. This was my job.

And even if I didn't sign up for it by myself, the universe did, and that was enough for me.

I walked into the circle of chaos that the guys had created, ducking underneath chunks of rock that were suspended in the air and hopping over streams of water that Apollo was about to use as a weapon, until I stood directly in the middle of it all. Every way I turned I was met by one of their angry faces, and I studied their expressions, each one as pain-filled as the last, and I couldn't help but feel for each of them.

You could see it written in their faces, but still, none of them compared to the passionate anger that was plastered across Apollo's, it was his signature style.

It was like his calling card, what he did best, and he was really doing it.

I stood in front of him, at the perfect angle so that his gaze would match mine.

I was no stranger to feeling his hotheaded wrath, and I wasn't afraid to throw it back at him, but this was different.

It wasn't just wrath, it was a look of pure pain engraved in his eyes. I turned to Adler and saw nothing but sadness, Atlas's was mixed with confusion, and Asher was a combination of all three.

I couldn't leave them like that. I didn't care how much they annoyed me, or how many times I tried to push them away, keeping them frozen in emotions that would tear them apart was cruel. Holding them hostage in the moment that they found out that the woman that they used to love was sleeping with each of them behind each other's backs was inhumane.

I didn't care if they wouldn't remember being stuck like it for so long,

just the thought of it almost broke my heart.

And that was the reason my backpack started glowing a light shade of blue.

I glowed brighter and brighter as the clock did the same until a small wave of energy burst out from it and washed over all four of them.

They rushed forward all at each other like not a second had passed, and I stood in the center of all the dangerous action.

I panicked, I hadn't thought it out completely, and I was about to get ripped to shreds before they even realized what they were doing.

"Stop!" I screamed at the top of my lungs. Two huge bursts of air flowed out from them and blasted them backward, sending them spiraling to the ground.

I could feel it drain a lot of my power, and I almost buckled at the knees.

"Holy shit Eden! What's your problem?" Apollo yelled back, a look of shock on his face.

"My problem?" I bent over and panted, trying to catch my

breath.

I rested my hands on my thighs and felt them quake underneath me, but I refused to let them give.

"The real question is what are all of your problems?" I said, finally getting back some of the fire that burned in the pit of my stomach. "I mean look at you! You're about to tear each other apart over something that happened so long ago."

"But-" Apollo started to say but I narrowed my eyes and held up a finger.

I knew how it worked. If I showed even a single ounce of doubt, he'd walk all over me. Not because he was a bad guy, but because no one had ever dared challenge him until I came along. No one stood up to him. He was used to being the head honcho, and he was going to have to learn that there was a new one in town. She may have been an emotional hot mess, but she wasn't about to be an emotional hot mess who let people go back to walking all over her.

"I'm going to need you all to listen, and listen well. I know you're all hurting. We all are. But right now, while we tear each other apart, there is someone out there burning the world to the ground wearing Asher's god damn face. Once we get to the bottom of that, I promise I will let you all tear each other limb from limb. But right now I can't let you do that."

Asher got to his feet and brushed the dirt from his pants. "With all due respect, how are you going to stop us?"

I smirked, a little scared at the rush of adrenaline that coursed through my veins at the fact that he dared to challenge me.

"I'm so glad that you asked."

I let my arms fall at my sides and took a breath. My left arm burst into flames and I used my right arm to pull a stream of water from the fountain nearby. Behind me I conjured a small tornado that lifted the dust and debris from the ground and tossed it in a funnel and a series of vines crawled out from the ground beneath me and arched into the sky.

It was the first time that I'd ever used all four elements at once, and if I was being honest I didn't know if it was possible.

But now that I stood there, holding them all steadily a rush of power washed over me.

I really was more powerful than I gave myself credit for.

I stared at Asher with the smirk still on my lips.

"Any more questions?"

Chapter Fourteen

"Tell me why we're here again?" Atlas asked as we stood at the edge of the desert, in the spot where it met the rest of the kingdom.

It was a strange transition. It went straight from lush green grass to dry beige sand, and there was no in-between. But I was beginning to learn that their entire realm was strange.

Our strange was their normal.

"Because the magical looking glass told her to, idiot." Adler smacked Atlas in the back of the head playfully, and I was afraid that I was going to have to break up another pissing contest.

"Because we need to get the other time clock for me to master the element, and mastering the element is the only way to fix the shit show reality that we live in. The time clock is somewhere in the ocean, and the ocean is past the desert, so here we are. Any other questions?"

I fanned myself with one hand and wiped a bead of sweat that slowly made its way across my forehead.

I could have picked a better time to freeze everything than when the sun was shining brightly.

But you live, and you learn.

The guys looked at each other questioningly, but none of them said a word.

"Great. We're all on the same page."

I rummaged through the bag, pulled out the telescope, extended it, and brought it to my eye. The invisible force turned me a little and straightened me out in the direction we needed to walk.

"Think of it as a map that only I can see."

"And we should follow you blindly why?" Asher mumbled.

I turned around and lit my arm aflame again, squinting in his direction.

"Because you have no choice." I offered an innocent-looking smile and a hair flip before taking the first step, tracking into the hot sand.

My foot slid across it, and I took another and another.

***

I hadn't planned on it being harder to walk in and taking up more energy.

I found myself using muscles that my legs didn't even know they had, not to mention the sand that somehow got into every crevice known to man. After a while of walking, I swore there was a thin layer of it coating my face and mixing with my sweat, even though the universe couldn't throw us a breeze to save its life. It wasn't long until I ripped the sleeves off the shirt that Silas had given me.

"Look out, guys, she's showing some skin. That means she means business."

I threw the strips of fabric that were leftover in the dirt and ignored him.

"Did anyone think to bring any water?" I asked, becoming increasingly aware of how my tongue felt like a wad of cotton in my mouth.

I had gone on such a tirade, I had packed my bag, and I had taken charge like a boss, but I forgot to pack food and water on a trip that we would have to take on foot.

Not very smart of me.

But I refused to let them see the crack in my armor.

"You mean you led us into the literal desert, and you didn't have any?" Apollo chimed in.

"I knew we shouldn't have followed." Asher groaned.

While it was nice to see them finally working on something together instead of trying to rip each other apart, I would have much preferred it not to be my last nerve.

"You know what? I was a little distracted by trying to keep you all from killing each other." I turned around and yelled.

I couldn't help it. I lost my cool.

But what I didn't understand was why the ground was rumbling underneath me.

"Guys?" I said, my eyes wide. My gaze flicked to Adler, but he shook his head.

"It's not me." He shook his head.

"And it's not me."

"Oh, no." Silas murmured.

"What?"

"Run." That was all he managed to get out before there was a loud noise from behind us, and a massive puff of sand exploded into the air and rained down on us.

If I didn't have sand in every crevice before that, I definitely did after.

"Holy shit!" Adler screamed, and we all took off, running as fast as our feet would let us in the soft sand.

My heart thudded in my chest, and I was sure my stomach had dropped into my shoes. I didn't know what the hell it was that exploded from the ground, but I knew that it wasn't anything I wanted to mess with.

"I can't see!" I yelled as I ran ahead, blindly rubbing at my eyes that burned. Sand had found its way inside and mucked them up so much that all I felt was pain.

"Help!" I screamed again as I ran, and after a few seconds, I felt someone come up from beside me and grab my arm.

"Move your hand." Apollo commanded, and as soon as I did, I

felt the cold embrace of his water flush my eyes.

It was the most relieving feeling ever, but the thunderous vibrations that shook the ground as whatever it was behind us chased us down was enough to drown out whatever relief I was feeling.

"What the hell is it?" I screamed at Silas, who ran close behind.

"A sand crab!"

The second he said it, I glanced over my shoulder and saw it emerge from a cloud of sand it kicked up. It appeared like a monster, and I almost screamed at its size. It looked almost like a regular crab, except it was a bright hue of purple instead of red, and it was the size of a freaking elephant. It was quite easily one of the most horrifying things that I'd ever seen until I laid eyes on it's two large claws and their razor-sharp points.

It scurried across the sand with a precision that I would have been amazed at if it hadn't been trying to kill us.

"Holy shit!" Adler screamed.

"Do something, Adler! Can't you pull a wall of rock up or something?" I screamed.

"What? From underneath the sand? That would take way more energy than I have! I haven't slept in how long? And I'm dying of dehydration!" He yelled back at me, a little more flamboyantly than I had asked for.

Meanwhile, an ear-piercing shriek filled the air that made my skin crawl in ways that I didn't even know was possible.

It sounded like a bad sound effect from a shitty alien movie. In a film, it would have been laughable, but in real life, I almost shit my pants.

Just when I didn't think things could get any worse, there was another sand explosion nearby, and another one burst up from the depths of hell where they'd come from and scared the shit out of me.

"Holy fuck!" I screamed as I twisted my ankle and went down.

How damsel in distress of me.

There was a flash of light, and the next thing I knew, Silas had yanked me to my feet and dragged me forward.

"Can't you teleport us all out of here?"

"It's like Adler said, it would take too much energy. I have my limits too." His voice wavered with each step.

My chest started to burn too, and I was sure that my lungs were coated with an even thicker coat of sand than my face.

I had to think, and I had to think fast. I was the one that had dragged us into the desert without food, water, and with absolutely no understanding of the wildlife that lived there.

If I got us killed, I'd never live it down in the afterlife.

I spun around and used what little energy I had left to create a tornado. It was only about as tall as one of the crabs, but as soon as I did, it picked up enough strength and sand to flip one of them on its back.

It landed with a thud, its legs kicking and flailing in the air above it. It tried to flip over, but it couldn't leverage enough weight.

"That's what I'm talking about!" Apollo screamed.

He was so proud of me that I couldn't help but smile.

And that's when my legs finally gave way, and I bit the ground, my entire face flopping into the sand.

"Shit!" Apollo yelled.

Atlas conjured a tornado too, and it swept up sand as mine had. Still, it wasn't enough to knock the crab entirely over, so Asher moved in and blasted it with what little fire he could muster, and after a few seconds, it exploded, detonating like a bomb and gushes of crab guts and pieces of shell were scattered all over us.

"What- the- Fuck!" Adler screamed at the top of his lungs, scrambling to brush off the purple goo from his skin.

"What the hell was that?" Apollo asked me as he pulled me from the ground.

"It's nothing. I'm fine." I mumbled, trying to keep myself from throwing up everything in my stomach onto the ground.

"Nothing? Eden, you almost blacked out."

"I said I'm fine." I pushed Apollo away and tried to walk on my own, but my legs wouldn't let me, and Apollo had to lunge to keep me from getting another face full of sand.

Atlas slung one of my arms over his shoulder, and Apollo did the same, and they helped me hobble forward.

"We have to keep moving. Who knows how many more could be out there."

"A lot, actually." Silas chimed in.

"Thanks, captain obvious." Apollo rolled his eyes. "Which way, Eden?"

I nodded my head in the direction we had been heading, but even that took a lot of energy. I felt so drained that I almost couldn't keep my eyes open.

I didn't know how I would do it, just keep swooping in and saving the world, if you could even call it that. But my mind kept traveling back to my father and what he had said.

The excitement in his eyes and the passion in his voice was enough to convince me to keep going.

I may have felt defeated at the moment, but I know that it would pass, and I refused to let myself stay that way.

I glanced over at Apollo through my tired eyes, and he half smirked awkwardly. "Don't worry. We'll get you to a safe place, and then you're going to rest. Got it?"

Only he could find a way to make a sweet gesture sound like a command, but I knew he was coming from a good place. He was sweet, but he just didn't know how to express himself like that.

Coming from one damaged person to another, I knew that it was rough trying to unlearn what life had taught you at a young age. There were some lessons that heartbreak embedded in you that were hard to forget.

If there was one thing I knew about Apollo, it was that he was genuine. Everything he said came from the heart. It was especially true when he didn't like someone, which was how I knew it was true when he did.

"Just hang in there, Eden. We're almost there." He said the words even though I was positive he didn't have the slightest clue where we were going, and that's when the ground beneath us started to rumble.

I thought it was another crab coming through, but I knew we were in deep trouble when the ground opened up and swallowed us whole.

Shit.

Chapter Fifteen

My lungs ached and my back hurt from the harsh fall. They erupted in a fit of coughing before I could even manage to open my eyes. The burn spread throughout my entire chest and felt like sandpaper carving out my insides.

I was buried in the sand.

I didn't dare open my eyes. And what little breath I had. I held on to as tightly as I could, which only made the burn worse.

My mind was racing almost as fast as my heart, and for a split second I was petrified with fear.

I'm going to die. This is how I die, and all the fighting I've been doing will all be for nothing.

I wallowed for a single second, ready to welcome my fate. I was exhausted. I was worn down, and all I could feel was pain.

I wanted it all to end.

Until I remembered meeting my father, and what he had told me about it being the eden's job to hold the peace.

If I was the last eden, and I wondered what would happen to the world?

It had already fallen into a state of disarray just from the few years I hadn't known who I was. Could I really let it fall even deeper down the rabbit hole?

If I died I knew for a fact that the other Asher would win.

He would burn the world to the ground, enslave all the castes, and ensure that the fire mages ruled.

And I knew that would have broken my father's heart.

I didn't know where he was, past or future, but I knew I'd meet him again one day, in this life or the next, and I didn't want to have to tell him I was the one that let the world go up in flames.

Not his daughter.

The ache in my chest spread to my head, and a stabbing pain developed behind my eyes, like little needles prickling across them.

I knew I didn't have much time until my body betrayed me and took in a deep breath on its own.

When that happened, I knew I would be done for.

The ache spread but something else rose up too, a fluttering feeling in the pit of my stomach and an icy feeling on my skin. I knew it was my powers bouncing around, trying to figure out a place to go, and I needed to use that.

With every ounce of power that I had left inside of me I let it flow out of me and into the world, the only thing on my mind that I needed it to get us out of the mess we were in. The energy surged out of me in a final blast that was so deafening that it made my ears ring.

Around me I felt the sand rising up, and up, and up, until I was free. It didn't surround me anymore, and it couldn't have happened at a better time because my body involuntarily took in a breath.

It was scratchy and it hurt like hell, but I didn't get a lung full of sand, and for that I was grateful.

The oxygen-filled my lungs and I felt like I was coming back to life.

And for once, I was actually thankful to be alive.

I brushed the sand from my face as well as I could and opened my eyes, blinking frantically to free them of the little sand that was left behind, and to adjust to the leery darkness that surrounded me.

I didn't know where I was, but it smelled damp and old.

Beneath me was a cold floor of rock. something that I was grateful for after walking the scorching rays of the sun for so long.

I used my power to light my index finger like a candle. It wasn't much but it was all I could do after feeling like I got the shit kicked out of me.

It was enough to shed a little bit of light on the thick darkness that surrounded me, which was just enough to see Apollo beside me, lying lifeless. Not far off were the others, scattered about and hacking.

They slowly got to their feet and rubbed at their eyes.

I pointed above us at the ceiling of sand that was being held up by nothing but my power, something that I was sure I couldn't hold much longer.

"We need to hurry." I said, my voice hoarse and raw. "I can't hold this much longer."

Silas nodded, and he and Adler grabbed ahold of Apollo. I tried to get to my feet but my legs refused to comply, and I was sent spiraling back down. Atlas and Asher caught me just in time and managed to help me move further down the corridor, or whatever the hell we were in.

I looked up to the ceiling and breathed a sigh of relief when the sand turned to the rock ceiling of a cave.

"That must have been what caved in." I said, my voice nearly a whisper.

As soon as Adler and Silas got Apollo out of harm's way I released the sand that towered above us and it crashed back to the floor, dust flying every which way.

We all covered our mouths and let the dust settle.

"How the hell did you do that?" Adler asked with his eyes wide. "No earth mage has ever been able to work with sand. It's unheard of. Not even the greatest ones."

"Well the greatest ones aren't me." I said as a reflex before motioning them to bring Apollo to me.

Asher had found a stray stick and lit it as a torch before sitting beside me.

Apollo lay lifeless in front of me, not moving a muscle.

"What the hell is wrong with him?"

"He probably breathed in sand." I said with tears in my eyes.

Suddenly the possibility of losing Apollo became very real to me.

He was a crab ass, and a dick, and sometimes I wanted to be the one to kill him, but I didn't want him to die for real.

I hadn't known him for long, but the thought of having to navigate the world without him raining on my parades was too much.

I didn't want to have any parades if he wasn't there to rain on them.

And I wasn't about to let him get the last laugh by saving me and then dying.

He wasn't going to get rid of me that easily, no matter how hard he tried.

And maybe it was selfish of me, maybe I shouldn't have wanted him to stay alive just for me, but it was the truth.

Because I loved him.

Every angry, grumpy part of him. He was the person who had shown me my real purpose. The first person to believe that I could be something in life, even if he tried to deny it.

And I wasn't going to let him die without seeing me live up to that.

The tears slid down my cheeks in muddy streaks but I didn't care.

I held my hands over his chest and let them hover there while I called on what little strength I had left in my body.

I took a deep breath and conjured up whatever I had left. A faint icy feeling climbed down my arms. It wasn't much, but it was better than nothing.

I tried to concentrate on the sand that I knew was holding him hostage, and tried to match my vibration to it.

I didn't know if it was the right way to do it, but it was what my gut told me to do, and if I'd learned anything it was that the gut of an Eden held knowledge that no one else did.

My instincts had led me through some pretty scary shit, and I knew it would do it again if I gave it a chance.

With my hands over Apollo's chest I tried with all of my might to pull the sand from inside his body.

"Tilt his head back and open his mouth." I managed to squeeze the words through gritted teeth.

The guys all looked at each other confused, but Adler rushed to his side.

I realized that there were tears running down his cheeks too.

Even after they had tried to rip each other apart I realized that the guys all had a bond that went back further than I could ever really know. They had known each other for so long that they were past the friends stage.

They were honorary brothers.

And I wasn't about to let Apollo die in front of them.

Adler opened Apollo's mouth. His body was still limp, but it worked in our favor because I was able to start pulling a stream of muddy sand from his body. It made its way out of his throat like a slimy mess, and there was a lot more than I had anticipated, but I was determined not to stop until I got out every grain that I could.

I would have gladly died doing it if I had to.

Dying underneath a pile of sand in the middle of nowhere was a no-go, but dying to save the life of a friend?

That was one hell of a way for an eden to go out if they had to.

I knew that would have made my father proud, and that was what mattered.

So when the stabbing pain crept its way up my spine and into my skull, I wasn't worried.

I wasn't anxious or afraid. My only concentration was getting enough sandy muck out of Apollo's lungs to bring him back in time.

All the other guys stood huddled around me as I worked.

All of their eyes shifted between Apollo's lifeless body, and me with awe.

But for once I didn't squirm under the attention of them all.

I didn't flinch, or even bat an eye.

I was consumed by one thought and one thought only, saving Apollo.

After a few moments the muck started to become sparse. I tried and tried but I couldn't pull anymore out.

I wasn't sure if it was because I was too weak, or if it had all come out, but it didn't really matter. The fact of the matter was that was all we were getting out, and it was time to get his lungs working again.

"Atlas." I snapped my fingers in front of his face, which broke the trance he seemed to be stuck in, staring at me with a look of surprise on his face. "Come back to earth Atlas. We're running out of time."

He nodded.

"I need you to use your power to funnel gusts of air into his mouth."

Atlas saluted me like a soldier and took his place beside Adler.

"Asher, you're on chest compressions. We can get his lungs pumping all we want but it's going to be useless if his heart doesn't join the party."

Asher stopped for a second, and I wondered if he was going to dare question why he should listen to me like he had when we were up top in the desert.

I narrowed my eyes at him, daring him to.

I'd use my last bit of power to knock him into next Tuesday if his stubbornness was the reason we lost Apollo.

We already had one cocky asshole in the group.

I didn't think that I could handle two.

After a moment he complied and made his way to Apollo's side.

I watched as he started compressions and Atlas gave him rescue gusts of air every few seconds.

I appointed Silas to oversee it and I stepped back, on edge, waiting to see what was going to happen.

After a few seconds I started to lose hope, until Apollo started to cough.

"He's alive!" Adler shouted with a smile on his lips.

A wave of relief swept over me.

It worked.

I felt like it wasn't just Apollo, I could breathe easier too.

Adler turned to me and the smile was wiped off his face.

"Eden, your nose." He said, concern flooding his eyes.

I brought my hand to my face and felt a gush of blood trailing from my nose down toward my lip.

And that's when everything went black.

Chapter Sixteen

I was swimming in a sea of darkness, but I didn't care. It was the kind of darkness that's cold embrace was better than the ache of breathing.

You never realize how much work it takes for your body to stay alive until it tries to stop.

I didn't know where I was, but I didn't mind because I knew that I'd saved Apollo. My good deed had been done. He saved me, and I saved him. We were even.

So I took a breath and let myself rest.

I deserved it.

***

I woke up like I was, encased in the black darkness.

I couldn't see a thing, but I knew I was inside of something because of the way that the air felt.

I reached out, and my hands were met by a smooth cold rock on all sides, like a coffin.

A stone coffin.

"Hello?" I called out, but the stone walls swallowed my voice. "Apollo? Adler? Anybody?" I pounded my fist against the solid wall.

Nothing.

I groaned.

Maybe I was dead, and this was hell.

Maybe this was what my eternity was destined to be. Cold and alone, trapped in a stone box of my fear- solitude.

For a second, I almost spiraled. I almost let myself fade into the darkness and give up.

But then I remembered who I was- what I was capable of.

I felt a lot stronger than I had before. I wasn't sure how long I had slept for, but it had done my body some good.

So I calmed myself. I took a deep breath and let my nerves fade into the background like white noise, concentrating on nothing but the low thrum of my heart beating inside of my chest.

As long as that heartbeat rang in my ears, I was alive.

And as long as I was alive, I had a chance to turn my life around. My circumstances didn't have to define me, and they wouldn't if I didn't;t let them.

I took another breath and brought my hand back to the smooth rock. I listened, not with my ears this time, but with my hands.

I used my power to blend with the rock-become it in a sense, and when I did that, I started to feel the vibrations. The low hum that made its way through from the outside. It took me a few seconds to realize that it was the vibrations of people talking-the guys.

I hadn't been transported to some weird and twisted torture chamber. Wherever I was, they were there too, and just knowing that made me feel a little bit better,

I took a breath and let my power flow from my hands and into the rock, blasting it out and sending debris flying in every direction.

I covered my face and let it fall around me, a cold gust of much fresher air washing over me.

"Holy shit!" A voice came from nearby.

It was Apollo.

I sat straight up with a smile on my face at the sound,

"Apollo! You're okay!" I climbed out of the odd rock chamber that I had been encased in and rushed to where he was sitting on the ground. I could tell by the look on his face that he had thought I would stop or at least slow down as I reached him, but instead, I tackled him straight, wrestling him to the ground with a hug.

He tried to push me off, like the grumpy asshole he was, but I didn't care and hugged him. There was a part of me that had thought I might never get to see him again, so the wave of relief that washed over me was the best feeling in the world.

I straddled his body as he was on the ground, and so many emotions were washing over me. Apollo looked up at me with a smirk on his face.

"I thought you were going to be trapped in that fucking stone cocoon forever. " He gestured over to where I had been laying. "You were like a caterpillar or something. You passed out, and then that thing swallowed you. We tried to get you out, but it was no use, so we built this fire, and we waited."

I smirked.

"You waited for me? You? You're not the waiting type." I teased.

And before he could say a word, I leaned in and brought my lips to his, kissing him with so much emotion and passion that a tear slid down my cheek.

"Ooooh." All the other guys chimed in simultaneously like they were in grade school.

And in the light of the small fire that blazed nearby I swore that I could see Apollo blush.

Bug bad Apollo, who was never embarrassed or afraid of anything, and my clit twitched at the thought.

I smirked, and a look came across his eyes like he knew what I was going to do.

The redness of his cheeks rubbed me in a way that he hadn't before, or maybe it was just the fact that I was so happy to be alive- so happy that he was.

Either way I got to my feet and walked over to Silas. I knew his eyes were glued to my body as I walked away from him, I could feel his stare.

I walked up to Silas, grabbed him by the back of the neck,

and pulled his face to mine, our lips brushing together slowly and sensually, and I knew Apollo was eating up every inch of the image.

And my panties were getting wetter just knowing that.

I didn't give a shit that we were trapped in some cave, or that the only light that we could see by was the fire that they had made.

Why?

Because we were all alive.

We were all there, living in the moment, breathing, and if the last few days had taught me anything it was that not everyone got to say that.

Not everyone got to make it to tomorrow, and there was no telling when any of us would have to leave this world and go on to the next.

All we had was now, and that was something to celebrate.

But even more so I felt bad that they were all heartbroken, all at the same time.

I wanted to show them that not every girl was like that. Not every girl wouldn't be honest about sleeping with all of them.

Silas kissed me back without the bat of an eye, slipping his hands around my waist and pulling me into his body.

He didn't question for a single second what I was doing, he was just happy to be included.

We kissed for a few seconds while the other guys stood there, awestruck. I could feel his cock slowly getting harder, the bulge brushing up against my thigh and making my heart race a little faster.

I pulled my lips from Silas's and turned to Apollo with a smirk.

"What are you doing?" Apollo asked, with a smirk equally as devilish.

"Showing everyone how happy I am that we're alive." I winked as I slowly inched toward Atlas.

His expression was hard to read, he wasn't completely smirking, but he wasn't frowning either. It was more like he was waiting in anticipation.

I brought my hand up to his face, and dragged my fingertips across his sharp jawline, his eyes locked on to mine, and his dark skin glistening in the firelight.

He leaned in slowly, expecting a kiss, but instead I let my fingertips fall, and glide across his muscular chest. Even with his shirt on I could feel the dips and curves of his toned body, and it only made me wetter.

When I made it to the waist of his pants I slid a hand in and wrapped my fingers around his semi-hard cock and smiled as it got harder in my hand.

I heard one of the guys gasp behind me, and another laugh, but the whole time I could feel Apollo's eyes locked onto me.

I glanced over my shoulder to make sure that he was enjoying the show, and the glisten in his eyes told me that he was.

He had come a long way from when we'd first had sex and the thought of sharing me with anyone else repulsed him even though he understood that I wasn't his possession and was okay with it.

But now it moved further away from the realm of being okay with it and into the realm of enjoying seeing it.

He still laid in the same position on the ground, but his cock was so hard that I could see the bulge from where I was standing.

I loved it.

Being the center of attention felt different now. The fact that they were all just alive and breathing enough to have their eyes on me made me feel so many emotions at once.

Atlas took in a little gasp and closed his eyes as I slowly started to stroke his cock inside his pants, and he quivered beneath my touch.

I stood on my tiptoes and brought my lips to his cheek, planting a single, innocent kiss before pulling my hand from his pants, and moving on to Adler.

Adler had to be the only one out of the others that didn't seem shocked.

Instead he stood there with a playfully excited smile on his face, the one that lit up the room.

That was what I loved about him, and it was what made me want to drop down to my knees in front of him with my mouth wide open.

I looked up to him as innocently as possible, my eyes big and innocent, with just a hint of mischief inside them.

By the time I made it to him his cock was already hard and at attention, so when I pulled the waist of his pants down it sprang up and practically slapped me in the face.

It felt like it had been so long since I'd felt Adler inside of me, even if it wasn't very long at all, and all I wanted to do was have him fill me. It didn't even matter which hole.

I grasped his cock, and gave it a few strokes before welcoming it into my mouth, letting it slide to the back of my throat.

Adler wasn't frazzled at all, and I even felt his hand come to the back of my head and his fingers tangle in my hair.

He wasn't being shy at all. He didn't even care that his cock was out for the other guys to see.

He leaned his head back and let out a confident moan, and that only added fuel to my dick sucking fire.

I used my tongue to caress the underside of his cock as it slid out of my mouth and I felt his entire body shiver in response.

It made me feel so powerful being able to bring one of the strongest earth mages known to man to his knees with nothing but my mouth. I got to feel him at the mercy of my throat, his cock begging for more.

But, much to his sadness, I pulled it out of my throat, got to my knees, and smirked as I made my way over to Asher.

There was a look in his eyes that I almost didn't recognize. It was half afraid, and half excited, and I didn't know which I liked more.

In all honesty, I wasn't sure if I was going to include him in the fun or not, but when our eyes met something happened that caught me off guard.

We sparked- again.

It was the tingling magic that I'd felt before, the magic that solidified the connection of soul mates.

And before I knew it Asher was on top of me, his lips on mine, with all the guys watching.

Well that turned out differently than I'd imagined.

Chapter Seventeen

Asher kissed me like he'd known me his whole life.

Like a lover that he hadn't seen in a lifetime, and there was something there lingering just below the surface of my chest that bubbled with familiarity.

It made my lips tingle and my heartache.

The more he kissed me, the more the shock wore off, and I kissed him back, the rest of the world fading to black.

I barely remembered the other guys were still there because of how my body felt beneath Asher's.

His hands roamed me. Not a single inch of my skin was spared from his touch, and I realized at that moment that there was no way he was the same person that I'd met earlier.

There was no way my instincts would have let this happen if it was. I had learned to trust them more than I could trust my own eyes.

So as he kissed me, I closed them. I forgot where we were or what we were doing. I even let *who* we were slip through the cracks. Everything fell to the wayside until it was our souls coming together.

And I couldn't feel it, the nagging ache of evil that I usually felt in the presence of the other Asher.

And that was when I came to accept that there was something else going on. Something bigger than me, or him, or the other guys, and it was my duty as an eden to add it to the fucking list of things that I had to conquer.

I felt his hand slip underneath my shirt, and his fingertips grazed against my bare skin. It sent a shiver down my spine, but the kind of shiver that gave me butterflies.

Asher pulled away from my kiss and leaned in close to my ear.

"Do you know how hard it's been for me to keep my hands off of you?" He whispered the words so softly that I knew none of the others had heard it.

It was a moment of vulnerability between him and me, and I believed him because I felt it too.

I was supposed to hate him- despise him, in fact, but ever since he'd stumbled from the doorway, it was hard for me to keep my eyes off of him. It had taken me that long to figure out why.

It was layers of sexual tension masked in stubborn confusion.

But there, beneath the glow of the fire, with all the others watching, it melted away, and I saw it for what it truly was.

A mystical connection that neither of us could control.

What we could control was how we handled it, and I was sick of ignoring it.

I could tell by the bulge in his pants that he was too, and that was music to my ears.

He brought his lips back to mine and his hand found the soft skin of my breast, squeezing a gentle moan out of me.

His hands on my body brought up sensations that I didn't know I had.

All the guys had a way of doing that to me.

Asher lifted my shirt and pulled it over my head, leaving me bare and exposed, my back against the cold rock of the cave floor.

I didn't care, though. It gave me a rush of adrenaline that made my eyes roll back softly.

Asher pressed his warm lips against the tight skin of my neck and trailed his way down to my nipple, circling it with his tongue in a way that managed to pull another moan out from my depths.

I held my eyes closed and let myself melt into the pleasure when I felt a cock slip into the hand that had been lying at my side.

Asher still had my nipple in his mouth and was now nibbling on it softly, so I knew it wasn't him.

I opened my eyes to see Adler kneeling beside me with his cock out. I looked up at him with a glint of adventure in my eye. A wave of lust swept over my body that was unlike one that I'd ever felt, and suddenly the thought of taking more than one of them at a time wasn't such a daunting one. In fact, the thought rubbed me in all the right ways.

I tightened my grip around his dick and began to stroke it, slowly at first. The way he closed his eyes and a small moan managed to escape his lips was something that sent a fire of passion rippling through every cell of my body. I didn't think it was possible, but I felt myself getting increasingly wet just at the sound.

I turned and looked at Atlas, who still stood with his mouth hanging wide, a look of shock plastered to his face. With a single finger, while I still stroked Adler, I motioned for him to come.

He didn't even hesitate, and the smile on his face was almost as satisfying as the way that Adler sunk his teeth into his bottom lip as I milked him.

I felt Asher's fingers hook into the waistline of my pants and slide them down my legs, the cool air creating a trail of goosebumps down them.

If I was honest, It was hard for me actually to believe it was happening, but when I felt Atlas's monster of a cock in my hand, it helped solidify the experience.

Was I really about to let all five of them ravage my body all at once?

Hell yeah, I was.

I knew just the thought of something like that would have sent the old version of me into an identity spiral.

But the person I was now didn't even think twice.

I jacked Adler and Atlas off simultaneously in tandem, and they both squirmed beneath my grasp. My eyes landed on Apollo, who stood on the outskirts now, the bulge in his pants far too large for him even to begin to try to hide.

He raised a brow at me, and I raised one back at him before an involuntary gasp escaped from my lips at the feel of Asher burying his face in my dripping wet pussy.

He didn't start slow and shy like any of the other guys would have. He didn't ease me into it or test the waters.

No, he went in like he was ravenous, and my pussy was his last meal.

Like he was on death row, and he knew he'd never get to taste another thing again.

Like his life depended on it, and at that moment, with the tip of his tongue in a delicate dance with my clit, I realized that I hated him a little less.

I turned to Silas and gave him a nod.

I didn't need to say a word because he already knew, but even if I'd wanted to, the series of moans that crawled their way out of my throat wouldn't have let me.

I was in heaven, and I knew all of the guys were too.

When Silas took his place at my side, I opened my mouth wide, and he wasted no time slipping his cock into my throat.

The thing about Silas was, even with all of his mystery and charm, there was an instinctual prowess that pulled its way out of him during sex.

I'd noticed it from the first time his bare skin touched mine.

And that was what made it so hard to believe that I was the only person he'd ever done it with.

Maybe he was just naturally a sex god. I didn't know how those things worked.

But what I did know was that his cock was delicious, and I enjoyed every inch as he crammed it into the back of my throat.

It took a little concentration to jack off the two guys and suck off the third, especially as I writhed beneath the mercy of Asher's tongue.

But I felt something in each of them, something mystical. I knew it had to be their power, the same way I had felt it the first time I'd slept with each of them. It was like my powers fed off theirs, and intimacy was the most potent way to transfer it.

And boy, were we doing some transferring.

I felt myself getting there, close to the edge, and I knew I didn't want the fun to end. Now yet.

So I pulled Silas's dick from my mouth and moaned for Asher to stop.

He pulled his face frame between my thighs, his chin glistening with my sweet juice, and smirked.

"What's the matter? You can't handle it?" I could tell by the look in his eyes that he thought it was true, but in reality, the reason was different altogether.

"No." I panted in excitement. "I don't want to cum until I've felt every one of you cum inside me first."

My words sent a shiver through his body, and his eyes snapped up to meet mine, dripping with lust.

I turned to Apollo and nodded for him to join.

He made his way to me and stood beside me with a hungry look in his eyes. He leaned down and brought his lips to mine.

"You look so beautiful with a cock in your mouth." He whispered, and I moaned.

"I'd look more beautiful with your cock in my ass."

He cocked his head to the side with a surprised look on his face, like he wasn't sure if he'd heard me right.

But when I threw a wink in his direction, I knew he was sure of what I'd said.

I wanted to have them fill me in as many ways as possible.

With every second that Silas's dick was in my throat, I felt stronger, I could feel my powers solidifying, and maybe that would be enough for me to get us out of whatever hell hole we were trapped in.

But I was so depleted that I knew it would take all of them, a group effort, to get me back to where I needed to be.

And I knew they wouldn't have a problem helping out.

Atlas and Adler grabbed me by the shoulders in one swift move and lifted me in the air just enough for Apollo to slide underneath me. They didn't waste any time.

He reached around and shoved two fingers in my mouth and made me suck on them until they were wet enough to lube his cock up.

Then came the strange wave of pleasure and pain as I felt the head of his dick slowly press up against my tight hole.

"Now, take a deep breath because this is going to hurt a little." Apollo whispered, and the others slowly lowered me onto his dick. At first, there was nothing but pain, and I winced, shutting my eyes as tight as I could. But after that, I felt my asshole relax, and a strange pleasurable feeling ran through my body.

"There you go." Apollo moaned.

I took Adler and Atlas's cocks back into my hands and opened wide for Silas to slide back into my mouth. At first, it was an awkward feeling, trying to balance them all, but I got into a rhythm after a few seconds. Apollo held my legs and bounced my tight little ass on his dick, and the final piece of the pleasure-filled puzzle came when Asher slowly thrust into my pussy.

The feeling of being sandwiched between the two dicks, both rubbing up against orgasmic hotspots that I didn't even know I had, was unlike anything I'd ever experienced. They all worked in sync, and every time that Asher thrust into me, it bounced me on Apollo's cock. They basically played sexual ping pong, taking turns thrusting into me, their cocks nearly brushing against each other inside of me, all three of us getting massaged in ways that we'd never thought possible.

"I need you guys to fill me." I moaned. "Every one of you. Now." I demanded.

I needed them to know that it wasn't a question or an option. They had no choice.

The only choice they had was what hole they wanted to fill me with.

Asher looked at me with a fire in his eyes- a literal fire. His pupils turned a reddish-orange, and his hair lit ablaze too, and for a few seconds, he went hard. He thrust into me so hard that even Apollo had to stop for a second.

I felt Apollo's hands travel to the inside of my thighs and pry my legs open even wider, and my pussy opened like a flower for Asher to destroy.

I was peeled wide, and Asher took advantage, fucking me like it was his job. He even grabbed both of my shoulders and used them to leverage my weight down on his cock harder.

"Cum for me. Now." My eyes locked onto his, and that was all he could take.

He thrust one last time, his cock sailing into me balls deep, and I felt the warm rush of his cum filling my pussy.

He pulled out quickly with a smirk on his face, rubbed his hands together with satisfaction, and uttered a single word.

"Next."

Atlas volunteered happily, and faster than the cum even had time to drip outside of me, Atlas slid his cock inside of me.

He and Apollo bounced me back and forth, and I threw my head back in ecstasy.

Silas moved to Atlas's side and enjoyed the feel of my fingers wrapped around his cock.

All of the guys were so close to busting that I was afraid that they wouldn't make it. I didn't think that they would have the self-control to hold it in.

Apollo mumbled a few curse words underneath his breath as he rammed his cock into my ass, and I felt his body tighten beneath me before he released his load into my asshole.

"Next." He moaned in my ear, his breath warm against my skin.

Adler didn't waste a single second sliding underneath me, and they commenced fucking me harder than I'd ever fucked before.

Atlas's fingertips trailed up the smooth skin of my exposed stomach until his hand cradled beneath my chin.

With one smooth move, he held it firmly and turned my head in his direction, giving me no other choice than to gaze into his eyes as I felt him fill my pussy.

"Next." He winked and flashed his gorgeous smile.

He held my legs in the air just long enough for Silas to slip into his place and slide his cock into me.

I was too close to being thrust over the edge into orgasmic bliss. I didn't know if I would be able to hold out any longer.

But one look was all it took for Silas to know what I was thinking.

We hadn't known each other for long, but as I said, he loved puzzles. And people just happened to be a type of puzzle that he understood.

He glanced down at Adler beneath me and nodded again.

Simultaneously, instead of plowing me, they both held me still and somehow managed to ram their cocks deeper inside of me, grinding against me.

Inside I could feel their cocks massaging one another with only my body keeping them apart. Their heads slowly danced across one another, and Silas's massaged my g-spot too.

He leaned in closer, closing the space between us, and whispered in my ear.

"Cum for us, love."

I couldn't hold it in.

I felt myself tighten around his cock, and my body convulsed, which started a chain reaction to his dick twitching and dumping his load inside of me, which was the last bit of stimulation that Adler needed to dump his in my ass.

My head was filled with an explosion of passion-filled fireworks that erupted in my mind and made my entire body feel tingly.

I was on cloud nine, and somehow it felt even better when they both pulled out, and I could feel their juices seeping out of my pussy and my ass.

Inside I felt more than just the post-orgasmic bliss that usually settled in after. I felt a rising bubbling sensation of power that settled into the pit of my stomach. It was like slowly it was undoing all of the exhaustion.

I could feel my body absorbing what used to be their power and making it into something of my own.

And I'd never felt more powerful in my life.

I collapsed onto the floor of the cave, my chest heaving.

Then something that I didn't expect happened.

One by one, the guys each grabbed a piece of my clothing and made their way to me. Adler grabbed my panties and slid them back up my legs with a smile. Once they were on, he leaned in and kissed my forehead. Atlas did the pants, making sure they were on comfortably before he leaned in and planted a warm kiss between my eyes just like Adler had done. Silas slid the shoes on, and with a flash of light, appeared at my side and opted to leave his kiss on the back of my hand like a gentleman.

Asher helped slide my shirt over my head. Only this time, his cheeks blazed a bright red. It was odd to see someone that I had watched burn cities to the ground get flustered in my presence. But even he leaned down and planted a kiss on my cheek.

There was more to Asher. He had layers. And although my heart knew we were destined mates, and I'd let him into the deepest parts of my body, I knew there was so much I had left to learn about him.

The good version of him.

And I was ready for it.

Lastly, Apollo came through and pulled a hair tie from my wrist.

He sat me up as gently as he could and stood behind me, running his fingers through my hair a few times to get the tangles out. I didn't need a mirror to know that I had a serious case of sex hair.

Gentle and Apollo weren't two things that I was used to putting together in a sentence, but I liked it.

He pulled my hair into a ponytail and fastened it with the hair tie before taking my face into his hands that were planted on either side of my cheeks.

He pulled me into him and kissed me on the lips in a soft,

passionate show of affection before pulling away and smiling.

It wasn't a sarcastic smirk. It wasn't an edgy grin, but a smile. A genuine, happy smile. I wasn't used to seeing that etched among his sharp features, but I liked it. Mixed with the light that shone in his eyes, it suited him, and I would have been perfectly happy if it would have stayed there forever.

"Alright, boys." I got to my feet and winced.

Somehow they all simultaneously managed to jerk forward, like I was made of glass, and if I were headed to shatter, they would have all saved me at once.

"Oh, god. Please don't tell me that now because I let you all fuck me at once, you're going to start treating me like I'm helplessly made of paper." I groaned, but with half a smirk because it was kind of cute.

I could tell that they all felt a new sense of bond not only to me but to each other. That was something that they needed for more than a while.

"Because remember, I can still do this." I held my hand up and lit my entire arm ablaze.

It was obvious that I was stronger now than I was before. The flames were more vibrant, and even the heat that radiated off it was on another level.

They all relaxed a bit more, and I nodded.

"Now then. Where the hell are we?"

Chapter Eighteen

" There were rumors of caverns beneath the desert, but I thought
that they were nothing more than fairy tales." Silas said as he
eyes the cave around us excitedly.

"Well, that's nice. Can't you just do your fucking blinking magic
trick thing and teleport us out of here?" Apollo interrupted.

It was nice that he felt better, which was obvious by the rate that
his old attitude was multiplying inside him. Soon he'd be completely
recovered to his full asshole health.

But there were a few things that I wouldn't have flinched if he
magically had left behind, his habit of interrupting being one of
them.

Silas just laughed.

Like Adler, he was an easy-going guy. And half of the time, I wondered if he was just too smart to know when someone beneath him was trying to ridicule him.

Was that a blessing or a curse?

"I'd love to, but you see, I'm not invincible. There are limits to what I can do, and I'm running low on energy and sleep. Two things that I need to travel long distances or bring others with me." Silas's voice was so calm that it made me want to be calm too.

"So basically, your power is useless here." Apollo grumbled.

"To put it in caveman terms, yes."

"Okay, okay, guys." I intervened, prematurely cutting off the pissing contest that I knew was already brewing.

So much for the harmony and peace that I'd fucked into all of them.

And while I would have been all for stripping them down and fucking them a second time just to get it through the gorgeously thick skulls of theirs, there wasn't enough time.

Every second we spent in the dark, damp caves was a second too much for me.

Wait a minute. This cave is damp.

I slid my fingers across the jagged rock wall and rubbed my fingertips together, feeling the moisture that slid between them.

My eyes darted down to the fire they had created when I was unconscious that still burned. The sticks and twigs that it was made up of crackled underneath the heat.

"It's got to have an opening and an ending." I said, cutting off the start of another conversation between Silas and Apollo that I was sure was going to blossom into a one-sided argument.

I was stating the obvious, but at that point, we were so lost that the obvious was still a good start.

"Last time I checked, trees don't grow in caves. And the moisture is so different from the sand up top. So, in theory, if we just breeze through this and keep walking, we should get to an exit, right?"

I looked up at them. I was determined to get out of the hell hole.

I was trying my hardest not to think that we were trapped underneath; god only knew how many pounds of sand. Not to mention the fact that a section of the ceiling had already caved in, and that was the reason we were there in the first place.

For all, we knew the stability of it could have been compromised for miles. Every second we sat like ducklings was another second, it could all go to shit, and we could be buried by sand.

I'd been there once. I wasn't about to go there a second time.

Not if I could handle it.

"Are you sure you can't just blast us out of here, Eden?" Apollo was starting to make me think that he just didn't want to walk or something.

"Not if you didn't like the feeling of that sand in your lungs before." I winked.

The way that we had come was completely blocked in by sand. It poured in from the ceiling and had created a heap that was so big it blocked it off.

So heading the way that I suspected led back to the city was a no go, but I didn't even care. There was nothing there for us anyway.

"Wait, where's my backpack, guys?" I asked at the sudden, alarming realization that I didn't have the slightest clue where it was, except that it wasn't on my back.

I felt stupid for not thinking about it sooner.

What if I had fallen on top of it and broke the clock? What happened if the realities that it contained spilled out of its confines?

Two things that I knew I didn't want the answer to, but definitely not if it came the hard way.

"Don't worry, Love. I grabbed it after the fall." Silas tossed it in my direction, and my heart jumped from my chest.

I leaped to catch it and almost scraped my knee to keep it from hitting the ground.

After all the warnings that Silas had thrown my way, I thought that he would have been more careful with it.

I brushed the sand from it and flipped it open, silently holding my breath, praying to every deity that came to mind that the clock would be unharmed.

"Oh, thank god," I mumbled underneath my breath at the intact clock.

I pulled the looking glass from my backpack and put it up to my eye.

I couldn't see a thing, but it did its job and spun me in the right direction toward whatever it was that fate had in store for me.

To my luck, it was further into the cave, where the sand hadn't yet blocked off.

"Shall we, boys?" I winked in their direction and nodded before grabbing a stray stick from the ground and setting it ablaze like a torch with the fire.

"Hey," Asher called out to me and sprinted to my side as I made my way down the corridor.

The other guys slowly followed, but they had all fallen into a conversation about god knows what and were taking their time.

It was nice that they didn't want to kill each other anymore, and if the downside of that was that they dragged their feet, then so be it.

"Hey." I smiled back at him.

The second my eyes darted to his, his shot in a different direction, and his cheeks glowed red. I could even see it in the dim glow of the torch.

It was strange seeing him so smitten, seeing the way that I gave him butterflies that made him squirm.

Even more so than the fact that just a few minutes ago, he was balls deep inside of me.

"I just wanted to say sorry." He rubbed at the back of his neck, nervously.

His words caught me off guard.

"Sorry?" I raised a brow.

"Yeah. For what I did to hurt you. Or, what you think I did. I don't really know what to call it, but I'm sorry."

The words hung in the stale cave air around us, and I didn't know what to say. I didn't know if I was happy or sad that the apology had come because up until recently, my hatred for Asher and what he'd done was one of the only things that fueled my ambition to go on. Getting revenge on him had become my life's mission.

This? This fucked it up.

I stammered like an idiot, fumbling over my words until my cheeks burned red.

I must have sounded extra pathetic because Asher overcame his embarrassment to look me in my eyes and put a stop to it.

"It's okay. You don't have to accept the apology. I just had to say it." He let out a sigh of frustration. I could tell that there was a lot on his mind—many things that he wanted to say but just didn't.

A lot of pain in his eyes over things that, if what he was saying was true, he didn't even do.

It took a lot of balls to apologize for things that you didn't do. I knew because, for me, it took balls just to apologize for things that I did out of my own free will.

"Do you know what it's like growing up in a place that just suffocates you?" His eyes met mine as we walked, and I could see how hard it was for him even to finish that sentence.

Asher was guarded, that was for sure, and the anger was still there beneath the surface. He just had a better grip on it than the other one.

It made me wonder what had happened to make him like that. I knew that the element of fire itself was intense. It had a way of crawling into your head and taking control of your thoughts. I knew that from experience.

But anger like that doesn't come from nowhere, and up until then, I'd never really cared to wonder what was the root cause.

But if I knew one thing, it was toxic childhoods.

My mind flashed back to when I was young, and the Nuns that ran the academy would throw me into the pool just to let me drown because they swore up and down that all I needed to do was believe hard enough, and I'd unlock my abilities.

The fuckers had the right idea, but the execution was made up of pure evil and hatred toward anyone that didn't align with who they thought they needed to be.

I nodded. "I know a little something about it."

"I thought I recognized another tortured soul." Asher smiled meekly, and my heart nearly exploded.

His smile- his genuine happy smile that had nothing to do with the pain and suffering of others was something that melted my heart. It was such a wholesome and beautiful sight.

And I was glad I was there to witness it, even if it took nearly being buried alive in the desert to get there.

We walked on for a few moments in silence, but not the awkward kind. It was the kind of silence that was still and peaceful. We both had the entire world on our minds and even more on our shoulders, which was what made the silence warm and mutual.

"You know, you can talk about it." I finally said softly, shattering the silence. "The world is a shitty place, but it's even shittier if you don't have anyone to share it with."

Asher thought for a moment, probably trying to decide if he

should or not, but I could tell that it was something that had been eating away at him long before he ever met me.

He had ancient demons hiding in his closet, but maybe mine could play with his.

"It was my father, mostly. He had all these expectations of me, all these dreams of what I could become, including the ruler of the fire cast, which was an honor set aside for the firstborn of every line."

"Okay, what's the problem with that?" I asked, trying to follow. I thought that it was a common custom.

"I wasn't the firstborn."

My eyes widened, and I knew where it was heading before he even dared to utter another word. "Your sister was."

Asher nodded. "For the first time in our family's history, the firstborn wasn't a boy. Which I'm sure in a lot of places without a sexist, rage-aholic for a king wouldn't be an issue, but for us, it was. My sister grew up hating herself and everyone around her because she wasn't born a boy, and when I was born, she learned to project that hate onto me."

My heart sank when I heard the words, and for the first time in a long time, I got a glimpse inside Asher's head. For a moment, it was like his walls had fallen, and he was reduced to nothing but the sad little boy who was both hated and loved too much.

"I didn't blame her, though. By simply being born into a family that valued women less than men, I stole something that was her right, something that she deserved. What I do blame her for is what she became, what she let my father make her."

I couldn't even believe that I was talking to the same Asher, the same one who had pushed me to snap and burn down my house. The one that had slept with my best friend and laughed in my face about it.

They couldn't be the same person, could they?

"And they say I was the one to kill her." Asher added solemnly.

The broken look on his face made the answer to my next question obvious, but I dared enough to ask it anyway.

"Did you?"

"No."

He was telling the truth. I didn't know how or why my gut instinct believed him, but it did, and all that meant was an entirely new door to a thousand questions was opened.

Before I got a chance to ask another one, a strange rumbling noise came from behind us.

"Guys, did you hear that?" I glanced over my shoulder, and we all froze.

They all nodded in unison with a grim look of fear in their eyes.

Then came the explosive sound of rock cracking.

The ceiling was caving in, and there wasn't a thing we could do about it.

Chapter Nineteen

Silas and I exchanged horrified looks as soon as we realized what was going on.

"Is it the fucking crabs again?" Adler asked with his eyes wide. "Because at this point, I'm already so traumatized that I'm never going to be able to eat seafood again."

"No. The entire thing is caving in, and we need to go right now if we want to live to see the sun again." I said.

Almost on cue, a large chunk of rick behind us fell to the ground, and sand started to pour in. A huge cloud of dust was headed right for us.

In an instant, I used my power to create a gust of wind to send back in its direction to combat it, but I knew it was only a temporary fix.

At that point, the rumbling was coming from everywhere, the ground and the ceiling both.

There wasn't anything we could do but run.

"Run!" I screamed and shot in the opposite direction, pushing my legs to go as fast as they could.

The others followed behind me, right on my tail, but the wind that passed me put out my torch, and we were engulfed in a blanket of darkness that was so thick that I couldn't see enough to put one foot in front of the other, and almost tripped over my own legs.

I didn't know what to do, I knew I probably had a few seconds until the guys started to trip over themselves, and all it took was one person down for all of us to be under fifty feet of sand.

An idea popped into my head, and I ripped the hair tie from my hair, freeing the locks in the wind, and in a second, I used my fire magic to ignite it.

I had seen Asher do it, and it didn't damage it, so I knew nothing was stopping me from doing the same.

I felt the warm tingly sensation start at my scalp before it spread down the length of my hair, and before I knew it, I was like a human torch, my hair glowing in gorgeous hues of orange and red as it flowed behind me.

It didn't just burn. It burned brighter than the torch had and gave off enough light for the guys to see behind me and for me to see further in front of me than I'd been able to before.

I knew that it was crazy, but something came over me that made me feel more alive than ever. Running for my life wasn't the best time to realize that I felt like my most authentic self, but moments like that came so few and far between that I took it while it lasted.

Which wasn't very long because up ahead of me, a large chunk of the rock ceiling fell to the ground, and more sand started to pour in.

We were fucked.

But only if I let us be. At that moment, I chose to believe in myself harder than I'd ever done before. Maybe it was seeing the guys finally interacting together, or maybe it was brought on by the reminiscing of my childhood. Still, I decided to show the nuns the biggest *fuck you* that I could think of my accepting that I could do anything I put my mind to.

I was powerful beyond measure, and what I was putting my mind to was getting us out of the shitty mess that I'd gotten us into the first place.

Instead of slowing my pace as we hit the cloud of dust, I held my hands out in front of me and ran faster, mixing two types of my power- my fire and earth- I kept my hair blazing as I put my all into lifting the sand.

A wave of pain swept through my head that almost made me want to stop, but I realized that the cloud of dust that was headed for us didn't just stop.

I made it stop.

It was working.

I just had to try harder.

So with everything in me, I pushed the dust wall back and slowly began lifting the sand.

I ignored all the warnings that my body was screaming and pushed through the pain and the pressure, the gallons of sand that were spilling in through the hole slowing, and eventually coming to a halt before they started to flow backward.

Little by little, as I barreled toward it, the pile of sand got smaller and smaller until it was all filtered back through the hole. I finally stopped directly beneath it, my chest burning worse than when it was filled with sand.

I held my arms above my head, stiff as a board, and swore I could feel the weight on them like I was holding it back by nothing but my strength alone.

"Keep going!" I yelled as Asher started to slow down when he approached me. "Keep going! We need to get you guys out of here before I can let it go!"

He looked like he was about to argue and blow my mind by proving that Asher not only was the monster that I thought he was, but he was chivalrous too.

A fact that my mind was too tired to accept, so I narrowed my eyes and repeated it.

"Go! I'll catch up."

Asher thought for a moment before nodding and continuing down the hall.

I turned to watch him and realized a faint light at the end of the tunnel. I could see it shimmering like a small star, far off in the star, but I didn't care. That small twinkle of daylight represented freedom and life.

Two things that I had never wanted more desperately than I wanted them at that moment.

Atlas and Adler sped past me next, leaving Silas and Apollo.

The minute that they passed, I was ready to let go when a chunk of rock from the ceiling fell, and the boulder crushed Silas's leg.

A disembodied scream clawed its way up his throat and echoed off the crumbling walls.

Shit.

I took a deep breath and calmed myself.

I knew I'd only have a few seconds to time it correctly, and if I was even a few milliseconds off, we could all die- Silas included, and then all of the work and the fuss would have been for nothing.

That wasn't something I was about to let happen.

I exhaled and let go of the sand that I was holding in place while sprinting. I heard it hit the ground as it all flowed back down again, undoing everything that I'd worked so hard to accomplish.

I didn't care.

My focus lasered in on Silas, who was only a few steps ahead.

Apollo had stopped and was trying to lift the boulders, but it was no use.

It was too solid for even him and his rippling muscles to tackle.

But where men fail, women flourish, and I was ready to blossom like a flower.

"Move!" I yelled at him. "Let a woman handle it."

I winked in his direction, to which he promptly scowled at the ill-timed cockiness, but all I was doing was giving him a dose of his own medicine. I found it laughable that it worked his nerves.

I held my arms out and channeled my earth powers once again, and lifted the boulder as easy as if it were a pebble.

Which only made Apollo scowl even more.

"I loosened it for you." He threw in quickly.

"Thank you so much. I appreciate it." My voice quivered as I ran, leaned down, and scooped up Silas by the shoulder without skipping a single step. Apollo grabbed his other shoulder, and Silas screamed, his leg hanging limp.

Shit. I glanced down at it, and it made my stomach churned.

He was lucky it was still attached, and that was putting the bloody mess lightly.

Not to mention how bad it must have hurt for it to drag across the harsh stone floor.

But after a few seconds, the pain was too much to bear and Silas passed out, his chin falling to his chest and his screams finally stopping.

It was a relief knowing he wasn't in agony, but I knew if we didn't push harder, we were about to be in a lot worse agony too.

Up ahead, the light that was once nothing more than a small twinkle grew into a much larger beam, an opening at the cave. The light was white and pure enough to make my eyes water, but I didn't care.

As long as whatever was on the other side of it wasn't an immediate danger, I was happy.

I could faintly make out the figures of Atlas, Adler, and Asher up ahead. We were running so fast that we were gaining decent ground, especially considering how much of a head start they had, but I knew that I couldn't hold onto it much longer even after the energy that I'd absorbed from them. I would have been crazy to think that I would be able to blow through it at the pace that I was going.

And even as fast as we were running, the sand flooding in practically nipped at our heels. So much of the ceiling had caved in that now it was a miracle that the little bit that still hung over us was even putting up much of a fight.

We were so close to the light that I could almost taste it, and seeing the moving figures of Adler, Asher, and Atlas rush into it and cross the threshold took a lot of worry off of my shoulders and gave me hope.

I hoped that whatever was beyond it wasn't worse because I didn't have the time for any of that shit.

Just as the sand caught up to us and I thought we were goners, we rushed through the light and made it to the other side.

I had to shield my eyes from the light for a split second to let my vision settle, but when it did, my jaw dropped.

We had rushed through straight into a large opening within the cave. It was so big and so tall that for a second, I could have sworn we were outside. It was lit well because of strange lights that lined the ceiling of the cave.

And in front of us was a semi-circle of people, standing in a row, with guns in our faces.

On either side of the entrance stood a person with their hands out toward the corridor that we had rushed down. I didn't understand why until I saw the wave of sand rushing toward us.

It had finally caught up to us, and I was sure that we were goners until the people at the edges stopped the sand with their power.

Not only were they earth mages, but they were powerful enough to manipulate the sand, like me.

I watched them hold back the pressure of the sand and close the opening with rock until we couldn't even tell where the opening had once been, and the rock wall that surrounded started.

"Who the hell are you people?" I exhaled.

A woman stepped forward from the line, placing herself in front of the line. Her hair was silver, and she wore a sleek black suit like someone in the special forces would wear, like a spy. She had a headpiece in her ear and a pistol strapped to her waist.

"We were about to ask you the same thing."

Chapter Twenty

❝I asked you first," I said. The flames that once lit my hair had died down, but the determination that they burned with switched to my eyes, and my glare was hot and daring.

I was ready to fight my way through these people if I had to, but that was before Silas groaned.

He was hurt, badly, and there wasn't time to fight.

I had to do one of the things that I was arguably worst at- actually use my words.

The woman smiled, but it was a cautious one, and she held up her hand, signaling the line of people all to cock their weapons.

My eyes darted from person to person, lingering a little longer than I would have liked on the weapons that they held. I could tell that they were guns, but they were unlike any that I'd ever seen. They were sleek and black, with chrome accents, and they all looked fresh and polished with futuristic boxy designs, and even the way that the people dressed was different too. They wore tactical suits like the woman with the silver hair. They looked like they would have more likely been an elite group of trained killers than a random group of people living in a cavern.

My eyes made their way up to the woman's.

"My name is Eden Montgomery." The words finally left my lips.

Silas was running out of time, and I swore that I wasn't going to be the reason he died. I was in a better, more confident place, but I knew that I wasn't going to be able to hold that on my conscience.

A look crossed the woman's eyes, a strange and surprising look before she looked me up and down with a new set of eyes. Like she was looking for something that she hadn't been before.

The man who stood directly at her side with his weapon drawn let it fall a little and leaned in towards her.

"Could it be?" He whispered way louder than necessary.

"I'll be the judge of that." The silver-haired woman held her hand up in his face and silenced his words, immediately reminding him of his place, which I had gotten enough to gather wasn't to question her.

"Your friend looks like he's been hurt pretty badly. He needs to get to our medics right away before he bleeds out." She eyed the bloodied mess that was once Silas's leg without batting an eye, which wasn't an easy feat.

But I guessed for someone who so freely held weapons in strangers' faces and dressed like she was always ready for battle, it wasn't much.

She was right.

And as much as I hated to be at the mercy of other people, it was for Silas.

He deserved to live long enough to keep shirking his responsibilities as King.

Long enough to be able to actually take me up on his offer to become Queen- If I wanted to, of course, which I still had no clue about.

I eyed the soldiers once again, calculating our chances of winning just for fun, which was low, to begin with.

"Yes. Okay, please, just help him."

The woman nodded and gestured for the soldiers to take Silas from us. It made me uneasy when one of the bigger guys swooped him up and threw him over his shoulder like a sack of potatoes, especially when my shoulders ached more than I cared to admit just from carting half his weight.

A few of them circled behind us to keep an eye on the back end, no doubt.

I didn't blame them, we were strangers, and they were probably as cautious of us as we were of them. It was understandable.

But I wasn't about to let my guard down either. Not for a single second before I found out who these people were and what their intentions were.

I was done cowering, and I made a promise to myself that from then on, I'd always be in charge. Always one step ahead, even if the other people didn't think so.

With the weight of Silas off of me, it was easier for me to check out our surroundings, and I realized that what we were inside looked kind of like a cave inside of the cave, only the ceilings towered above us so high that it seemed like it could have been the sky.

Not only that, but the ground wasn't made of Stone anymore. It was made up of dirt and grass.

We were on the backside of a large, grassy hill, and at the top stood a tree.

"Holy shit. That's amazing." I gasped. "All of this is inside of a cave?"

I heard one of the soldiers behind me snicker at my amazement and almost got defensive until he spoke up.

"If you think that's beautiful, just wait."

The woman and the soldiers led us up the hill that was tall enough to block the view of whatever was beyond it, and when we got to the top, my stomach sank, but my jaw sank lower.

The soldier was right.

In front of me stood a huge futuristic city.

The ceilings were taller than I could have ever imagined, tall enough to fit large buildings, and the cavern stretched further than I could see. In the span of it were roads, and houses, parks, and ponds.

It was an entire city built underground, powered on technology that was so advanced that my realm's tech couldn't even hold a flame to it.

I knew that the second I spotted a car that hovered above the ground.

I didn't know what to say or what to think.

So I stuck with my tried and true catchphrase of *holy shit.* Mumbling it a few times over and over as we walked.

There were even birds perched in the trees.

If I hadn't known better, I would have sworn that it was a normal city up on the surface.

Minus the high tech, though.

"What is this place?"

"Welcome to the Den of Eden." The Silver-haired woman's voice trailed behind her.

For a minute, I thought that my ears were playing tricks on me until she turned around to gauge my reaction, and I knew that what I'd heard was true.

I could tell she was testing me, gauging my reaction, and I was under her microscope.

For as long as I needed her to co-operate to ensure Silas's life continued, I refused to give her anything suspicious to work on.

I knew the universe had a reputation for giving me a hard time, and I didn't plan on making its job any easier.

I held my hands down at my sides and followed like I was told to, but I twiddled my fingers nervously, ready to pounce at a moment's notice if I had to. I was weak, but I knew that the people that I loved were my weak spot, and I would go to the ends of the earth to save them.

If they needed me, my body would create the extra energy I needed, even if it was only for a second.

I stayed ready.

And in front of me, Apollo glanced over his shoulder at me. It was only a split second, but our eyes met, and I knew that he felt the same way.

There was no way anything sketchy was going to go on with all four of us there.

My only concern was getting Silas back to health and finding a way out of this place and back on our mission.

I could barely find it in me to trust one person, let alone to trust an entire city of people that I'd never met that was mysteriously located underground.

Everything about that screamed suspicious to me.

I tightened the straps on my backpack cautiously and tried my best to keep up.

Even though the entire city was located inside a cave, it was still surrounded by a large fence made of a strange glowing blue light. The fence reached all the way up to the ceiling, and the only way in or out was through a single set of gates that was heavily guarded like a military checkpoint.

As the woman approached, the guards on duty straightened their posture, and their hands flung to their temples in a salute.

"Madam President." They both addressed her.

President? The word rattled around in my head. Obviously, she was in charge, but I wouldn't have guessed on a presidential level.

"At ease, soldiers. We're headed to the infirmary. We have someone in critical condition." She said, her voice smooth and calm.

"Of course." They scrambled to open the gates, and after a few seconds, they slowly glided open.

"Keep up the good work." She said, and I couldn't tell if I'd actually detected a level of cheer in her voice or if I'd made it up.

Either way, there was definitely a difference in the cold and calculating tone she used with us.

We passed through the gates, and the second that we did, they closed it behind us, sure not to waste a single second getting it closed again. It made me wonder what the hell they thought was going to make it through the tunnel that had completely collapsed, but it had them spooked.

Or maybe the president lady just had them whipped.

Either way, it made me wish even more that they weren't hostile and pray that they would just let us leave. I wasn't in the mood to fight my way out of anything, and I probably wouldn't be in the mood for a while.

If ever.

Inside we immediately crossed to a small building that lined the fence with a red cross on the outside to symbolize the infirmary. One soldier rushed ahead to open the door for the silver-haired woman to enter, followed by the soldier that was carting Silas.

Then they tried to close the door and deny us entry.

Asher, Adler, and Atlas all stopped and looked at each other confused, and I thought I would have to be the one to fight with them, but Apollo took it upon himself.

He walked up to the soldier that had closed the door and placed himself in front of the door and stopped only inches from him.

"Move." Apollo demanded.

The soldier was short, but he was muscular. You could tell that even underneath his slick black tactical outfit. He stood with his hands clasped behind his back, and his chest puffed out.

His gaze was relaxed and unwavering like he was focused on some invisible point on the horizon, almost like Apollo wasn't even there.

"I said move." Apollo pulled a stream of water from his pouch and held it out threateningly.

"I have orders." The soldier responded coldly.

"And I have an urge to give you an ass-kicking. Your point is?"

"My point is, you're not getting in."

I could feel Apollo ticking like a time bomb, and I would have felt bad for the wrath that the soldier was unleashing on himself, but the way that the mages had lifted sand so effortlessly was insane.

I didn't know what kind of mages they all were, but I knew that Apollo would need some backup.

"That's cute. Surfacer." The soldier threw the insult like it was supposed to hurt us. Like we were supposed to know what it meant and let the offense roll in.

But instead, Apollo just stared at him blankly.

He raised his whip to strike, and in turn, the soldier pulled the cork on a bottle that hung on his side and pulled a stream of water from it too.

We were about to see the fight of a lifetime when the door swung open and hit the soldier in the back of the head, knocking him off balance.

"Ouch!" He yelled before rubbing at it to nurse his wound.

"Let one of them in." The President's voice came from inside.

"No. We're all coming." I rebutted.

"Then, he dies." She answered so quickly, and with such little regard that I knew she wouldn't hesitate.

And that was what scared me the most.

I glanced over at the guys, and they all ushered me to go.

"I'll keep my eyes on dickhead here." Apollo groaned.

I nodded and slipped through the door.

Chapter Twenty One

I made my way into the building and the door shut behind me.

Surprisingly the building wasn't as ominous and mysterious as I had imagined in my mind. I painted the image of a dimly lit torture chamber, with an assortment of chainsaws gracing the walls, maybe a few blades.

But instead, I was met with a sterile white room with a few hospital beds pushed up against the back of the room.

One entire wall of the room was covered with nothing but monitors that blinked across the screen.

There weren't any other patients, but there were three people in white coats huddled around the bed that Silas lay in, ripping off his clothes and strapping all kinds of wires to him.

My first instinct was to rush across the room and put an end to it until they explained to me what every one was, but I knew the more time I spent contesting them, the less time he had to heal.

And the injury to his leg wasn't just looking grizzly. With the amount of blood that he had lost, it was looking lethal.

And I refused to lose him.

Any of them, for that matter.

So I clamped my lips tightly and watched.

I trusted my gut to tell me when something was up. If there was anything I needed to be suspicious of, I knew that it would have my back. There was no need to worry.

Yet.

It was only a matter of seconds before they had cut Silas's shirt all the way up the center and had what was left of his pants off too, so he laid in his underwear while they got readings on his vital signs and got a better look at his leg.

It hurt just to look at it, and the second that I did, I swore I felt a gross feeling in my own legs like my body was trying to imagine what it must feel like- which was something that I really would have rather not known.

"How did it happen?" One of the doctors, a short blonde woman, turned to me.

"A boulder fell from the ceiling and crushed it."

"And how did you get it off?"

"I used one of my powers." I said.

I tried not to sound odd, but I knew the President's ears perked up the moment I said it.

She looked at me out of the corner of her eye, but still, she didn't say a word.

"Do you know his blood type? Or his birthday? Or anything?"

I shook my head, my cheeks sizzling with embarrassment.

"I haven't known him long."

"Yet, you were quick to nearly fight us all for him?" The President finally broke her silence and turned to me.

I knew the question was more of a rhetorical question and was probably aimed at charming me more than anything else. Still, I answered anyway because I refused even to give her the slightest chance to think that she had gotten under my skin.

She hadn't.

I just had more important things to think about, like Silas's recovery.

"Yes. And I'd do it again in a heartbeat, so I'd prefer it if you guys didn't give me a reason to tear this entire city to the ground. It would be a shame to have to see it burn."

I said the words with a voice of steel, unwavering, and strong. And my gaze was just as solidly glued to Silas's body.

I wasn't going to let them harm a single hair on his head.

And I wasn't going to let miss bossy distract me for a single second to give them the opportunity.

Out of the corner of my eye, I saw her smirk. I couldn't tell if it was because she was impressed with my will of iron or if it had evil intent, but either way, I was proud of myself for staying true to my mission.

I watched as they took a syringe and poked it into Silas's skin.

"What was that?" I asked.

"A healing mixture." The blonde doctor answered without looking back.

I respected her dedication to his care. Like me, her focus was lasered in.

And I had no complaints about it.

"What is this place?" I asked blankly.

"The infirmary." The President responded blankly.

"No. Like the entire place."

"The Den of Eden." She said again. "You really must not listen well."

"I'm sorry, I always find it a little hard to concentrate when I have fucking guns pointed to my head." I folded my arms angrily. "It's a flaw of mine."

"Nobody's perfect." She smirked.

I noticed that there were crows feet and smile lines etched fairly deep into her skin. It was hard to tell from far off, but up close, it was easier.

I took it as proof that she wasn't a robot and had smiled at least a few times in her life. But those two things didn't do much for me, unfortunately, because it was easy to kill someone and smile.

And I wasn't trying to get smile-murdered.

"Is he going to be okay?" I asked the doctor, tearing my eyes from the gruesome wound for a split second.

"Yes. But we need time to work, and he's going to need time to heal. You should move on and come back later."

I raised my hand to contest what she was saying, but I felt a hand on my shoulder.

It was the President.

"Hey, kid. He's in good hands." She said, daring to show the slightest bit of personality.

"It's not him I'm worried about." I said outright.

I didn't care if I was forward, or they thought I was rude.

The truth of the matter was they outnumbered us.

And I had places to be, world's to save, and curses to break- In that order.

"I'm not leaving him."

"Oh, how I wish I were asking for your permission to remove you from this building." She half laughed. "But I'm not. So you can either leave willingly, or you can leave the much harder, and quite frankly more embarrassing way."

She nodded toward the soldier in the corner that had carted Silas in like he was nothing.

She didn't have to say another word. I got the gist.

I didn't like it, but I understood it.

I took one last look at Silas. I knew the possibility of him hearing me was slim, and I'd most definitely sound stupid speaking to an unconscious person, but if anything ever happened to him, I knew that I'd regret that being the last thing he heard me say.

"I'll be back for you, Silas," My voice cracked. "Don't die on me, or I'll kill you." I laughed awkwardly to ignore the collection of tears that danced in my eyes and threatened to spill out.

"I promise you, he's not going anywhere. Nobody is until we figure out what's exactly going on here." She said once we made it back outside.

Apollo stood with his water whip still ready, the anger still as fresh in his eyes as it had been the moment that I had left him.

If there was one thing that I could count on Apollo for, it was always ready to head into battle, even if he didn't know why we were battling.

He was always ready to fight, and that was the type of energy that I could appreciate.

"Please, follow me, and I'll show you to your quarters while we straighten this out." She took one look at the thin layer of dust that seemed to cover my entire body somehow, and I knew that it was aimed at me.

Was it really my fault if saving everyone's lives was such a messy job? I didn't think so.

"You're so hospitable." I forced a smile.

I made sure to stay close to the guys. Not because I needed their protection, but because I felt like we made a better team when we were together.

And partly to give the backpack more cover.

The last thing I wanted was for them to find the time clock of the looking glass. I didn't know why I wanted to hide them so badly. My gut wasn't telling me that they were bad people. But it was telling me that the clock and the looking glass weren't in their possession for a reason.

There were so many things going on that I didn't understand, and Silas wasn't around to fill me on things that he knew.

I was left with nothing but me and my gut.

They led us away from the infirmary and down a cement walkway that led further around the city's outskirts. I was getting the feeling that the space near the edge of the border was reserved for the military because outside of every building, a soldier was posted, standing atent and ready.

I eyed each of them and couldn't help but notice that each of them carried three small vials on them on top of guns, a lot like the pouch of water that Apollo carried. One held water, the other held sand, and the last held small black rocks that looked like they'd been forged from fire.

I didn't know what the hell was going on with these people, but as we walked I promised that I'd figure it out, and I'd get us out of the place.

Chapter Twenty Two

W e were corralled into a strange vehicle that looked like a military truck, but it didn't have any wheels. Instead, it sat completely on the ground.

We were all ushered inside the back of it, and even though my heart raced at the thought of being confined in a small, covered space with the soldiers, I took a deep breath and forced myself inside.

It wasn't like I had much choice until I could figure out what we were up against.

Adler, Asher, Apollo, and Atlas all followed behind me, and inside took a seat on the bench-style seating beside me.

They refused to let any other soldiers near me, and I couldn't help but smirk at their protectiveness.

They knew I didn't need it, and if it came down to it, I'd be right next to them kicking some soldier all, but they chose to show me where they stood, and that meant more to me than they would ever know.

The President filed in next, followed by more soldiers until the door was closed behind us, and we were engulfed in darkness. There were no windows, and the outside of the truck was metal painted in a camouflage pattern.

The design itself didn't make much sense to me, but who was I to argue?

The truck shook a little as the soldiers climbed into the cab and a small humming vibration flowed through the floor as they started it.

We could feel the vehicle stutter on and then the rising feeling of it lifting off the ground to hover like the other cars we'd seen.

Then there was an electronic glow from somewhere on the ceiling, like the soft lighting that made up the fence, and within a few seconds, the walls around us disappeared like they'd become transparent.

The light that flooded in from around us was so bright that it took a few seconds for my eyes to adjust completely, but when they did, it was hard for me to hide my amazement.

We slowly started to move down the street, and we could see clearly all of the scenery passing us by.

"How is this possible?" I asked, annoyed that the impressed smile refused to leave my lips.

How could I not be?

"Advanced technology." The President smiled back at me.

If I didn't know better, I'd think that she was warming up to me.

"This is the kind of technology that people from every realm have tried to come and steal." She added quickly, her voice returning to its cold tone.

Okay, I know better.

I reached out to stick my hand out of the vehicle but instead, my fingers brushed up against the cold, smooth surface of it. It was trippy to see my hand pressed up against nothing. My brain told me that it was an invisible force, but I didn't believe it.

"Cameras?" I asked with a brow raised.

"Smart woman. Most would have thought it was a trick of air mages or something."

"Well, I'm not most people." I brushed off her compliment. She was a hard person to read, but if there was one thing I had had enough of in my lifetime, it was head games. I was sick of them, and after living with Jade and being manipulated by Asher- the wrong Asher, I wasn't about to let it happen again.

"The outside is covered with hundreds of microscopic cameras, and the inside is lined with screen technology that lets us see what's going on in the outside world. To them, they see a covered truck, but we see everything."

It was smart, I had to give them that, and the screen technology was more advanced than anything I'd ever seen.

The entire place was.

But I refused to let the nerd inside of me be impressed.

Growing up with absolutely no powers and only one friend left a lot of free time in my schedule, most of which was filled with reading science fiction that looked a lot like this.

But then again, hundreds of years ago, people being able to control elements was considered science fiction.

Anything was possible.

Around us, the scenery flew past, and I realized that the glowing shade of blue in the distance was the fence that surrounded the outskirts of the city.

We were headed into the heart of it.

After a few minutes, and the closer we got to the center, we started to see other hovering cars on the streets, and soon people were walking the sidewalks.

We stopped at an intersection, and I looked up in awe at the buildings that towered above us.

They looked as real as any modern city in my world. Stores and restaurants were scattered among them.

I tried my hardest to keep my guard up.

Sure they weren't what you would have expected to find in a colony of cave people, but that didn't mean they were good people.

They could have been evil for all I knew.

But then my eyes lasered in on a woman walking down the sidewalk, with a laughing toddler clutching her hand.

They both held an ice cream cone that they'd gotten from the shop on the corner, and they laughed and smiled as they walked.

The little girl's eyes were so bright, and she looked so happy.

Was that evil?

Could I really convince myself that it was?

I groaned.

I couldn't, and I knew it.

And there went my plan of despising these people for fuel and motivation to break out of it.

And if I didn't despise them, I was afraid that I might love them.

That was a thought scarier than anything else.

"So, how about you tell us who you really are?" The President said calmly. "We all can. I'll start. I'm President Kim Young. I run the den and make sure that everyone is safe and secure. These are all soldiers of the guard."

"I've already told you who I am," I mumbled. "Eden Montgomery. And this is Apollo, Atlas, Adler, and Asher."

"You said that, but I'm having a hard time believing that." President Kim smirked in the pettiest, polite way possible.

"Oh yeah? Why's that?" I had no problem throwing the shade back at her.

If she wanted to play that game, I had no problem throwing on a jersey and playing too.

She brought it on herself.

She didn't say a word. She just looked me up and down and whispered something into the soldier's ear beside her.

I didn't know why, but it made my blood boil. So I leaned in and whispered into Apollo's ear like I had something important to tell him too.

"She's a bitch."

Apollo burst out laughing.

I could tell he tried to hold it in but couldn't.

I didn't care, though. I hope it made her upset.

We rode the rest of the way in silence.

I knew if they were going to kill us, though, they would have already done it.

And they wouldn't have bothered helping Silas either.

So as it stood, they needed us alive, and something told me that it wasn't out of the kindness of their hearts.

I didn't care, though. I was going to use it to our advantage.

I didn't know how yet, but I trusted myself enough to do it.

The vehicle slowly came to a halt outside of what looked like it was the largest building inside the city. It stood like a skyscraper in the center of it. The building itself was a strange, asymmetrical shape that was oddly satisfying.

"Well, this is it." President Kim got to her feet and made her way through the doorway.

The guys and I exchanged looks. The look in each of their eyes was charged up. They looked like they were ready to fight as soon as I gave the word, and I didn't doubt it.

"At ease, soldiers." I faked a salute and laughed.

They didn't seem to find as much humor in it as I had, but we followed her out of the doorway anyway.

There were a few people that stood outside of the building going about their daily lives, but the second their eyes landed on me, their eyes widened like they'd just seen a ghost.

I didn't understand why they felt the need to gawk like that. Sure, I probably looked like I'd just gotten railed by five guys and then hit by a train, not to mention the layer of dust and mud that was caked onto my face and my clothes.

But even then, staring was fucking rude.

What were they, five?

It was like their world had come to a screeching halt the moment they saw me, and they began murmuring to themselves.

"Wow, is there something on my face?" I asked before I nudged the President with my elbow.

In my mind, it was a playful thing, and partially to piss her off.

But the second my elbow touched her, the soldiers flipped out, pulling their weapons.

I didn't flinch, but the citizens on the street looked mortified.

"What are you doing? Do you know who that is?" A man called out from further down the sidewalk.

At first, I thought the statement was aimed at me, to which I was about to reply that I knew very well that she was the President.

But instead, the President answered.

"Not yet, but we will soon."

I raised a brow before the soldiers ushered us inside the building. The two front doors slid open automatically for us. The transition was a smooth glide.

Inside was a large corridor that reminded me of the lobby in an upscale hotel, only way more futuristic. There were security guards everywhere, and in the center of the farthest wall hung a gigantic portrait of President Kim.

"Self-centered, much?" I groaned underneath my breath.

We were led through the lobby and past a girl who sat behind the front desk. Her eyes were just as wide and surprised when she spotted me like everyone else's.

"Is that-"

"Let us through." The President breezed past the front desk, and a small metal gate opened that led us to the back of the room.

The soldiers pressed a button that opened the doors of a see-through elevator.

There wasn't glass around it or anything. It was just a circular metal pad on the floor that rose to a circular cutout in the ceiling.

Beside it, I watched one of the pads descend back into its place on the ground, no strings or pulleys attached to it whatsoever.

Their technology was unparalleled to anything that I'd ever seen.

I could hardly believe it.

We were ushered onto the pad, and we all stood quietly as it rose into the air, and butterflies exploded into my stomach.

The city was turning out to be an even bigger mystery than I'd ever thought.

The pad rose and rose through so many floors that I'd lost count until we made it to the top floor. I knew it was the top because every other floor had a circle carved into the ceiling for the elevator to pass through. This one didn't.

"Show them to their rooms." The President waved in the guys' direction, and the soldiers grabbed them by the arms.

They started to fight, and I knew Apollo was about to lose his shit.

He'd been waiting for someone to do something so he could rip the place apart, but that was the exact opposite of what we needed.

It definitely wasn't what Silas needed.

"Hey!" I yelled.

Apollo froze with his fist in the air, aimed at a Soldier with a gun aimed at him.

"It's okay. Just go. I'll be fine."

All four of them looked at me, confused, and I threw a subtle wink in their direction.

They knew I had something up my sleeve, so they calmed.

But little did they know it was so secretive that I didn't even know what it was yet.

Chapter
Twenty Three

The soldiers carted the guys away. Despite their anxious looks, I knew that they would be okay. They were strong, and they didn't need me to prove it. They were around long before I was, and they'd survived. I trusted them to stay alive for a little while longer so I could figure out what the hell was going on in this place.

After they were carted down a separate hallway somewhere, it was just the President, one soldier, and I left.

She must have gotten brave to let all the others leave.

Either that or she realized I wasn't a threat, or imposter, or whatever the hell that she thought I was.

I still had the backpack strapped to me, and I watched every angle to ensure it was still safe.

If they were thinking stripping the guys from me would make me weaker, they had another thing coming for them.

And it wasn't a pretty thing.

"Now, without all of your buddies here, can we talk about why the hell you're treating us like intruders?" I asked, my voice gruff with a twinge of anger in it.

"Because you are." She said calmly.

Which technically was true, but she knew what I meant.

"Walk with me." She motioned as she made her way further down the hall.

I grumbled, but I complied and followed closely behind until I managed to catch up and walk with her at her side.

"The Den of Eden has been an operating city for over a hundred years." She said proudly. "We've survived this long using the knowledge of our founder, upholding our values, and strengthening our principles. There haven't been outsiders in the city since it began. That's how seriously we take our security."

I nodded.

It made sense, but I couldn't figure out why the hell she thought now was a good time for a history lesson.

We made our way further down the hallway.

Much like the infirmary, the walls were a clean and sterile white, with crisp white lighting lining both sides of it.

It all felt like it had stumbled out of an old sci-fi movie but in the coolest way.

Still, I tried to contain myself.

We walked and passed a few closed doors without handles. All they had was a keypad beside them that glowed a vibrant shade of blue.

"We learned from the dark times in history and treated their lessons like our own. We pride ourselves on kindness, empathy, understanding, and the knowledge that anyone can learn to master all four of the elements."

Those were the words that stopped me in my tracks.

I froze, and after a few steps, the President did too, turning to look at me out of the corner of her eye.

"Wait a minute. Everyone here can use all four elements? Everyone's an eden?"

The President chuckled like she thought my question was laughable.

She held up her hand and lit it ablaze before opening a pouch at her pack and pulling water from it. From the other pouch, she pulled sand out with nothing but her power and finally summoned a breeze to sweep through the hallway.

My jaw hung open.

"What the fuck."

She smirked at my word choice before she started up her pace again, and I hurried to catch up with a smile on my face.

"I thought I was the only one- I-" I stuttered, trying to gather my thoughts.

"You see why we protect the city at all costs?"

I nodded but only understood slightly.

"Wait, did I come from here? My ancestors or something?"

"Why would you ask that?"

"Because you all control the elements too."

"Yes, but anyone can do that if they learn. Our founder taught us that."

My stomach churned, and I wasn't completely sure why.

Maybe I was getting used to the thought that I was special, one of a kind, only to accidentally stumble across an entire city of people who were just as extraordinary as I?

But if everyone was extraordinary, did it slowly turn into just plain old ordinary?

"Your founder sounds like a smart person." I said simply because of a lack of better responses.

"She was."

The President stopped at a door and pressed her hand against the keypad. A small light scanned her palm before it changed from blue to green, and the door slid open to reveal a lavish apartment.

"Wow." I gasped. The entire back wall of it was glass, and it overlooked the entire immaculate city.

She walked in, and I followed, admiring the white decor as I did. There was a clean white piano with a bench that had golden accents beside the door. Straight ahead was a small dining room area that opened to a large kitchen and off to the side was a room with a bed that I could just barely see.

For kidnappers, there were probably worse places that they could have stuffed us.

And I was grateful for that, at least.

I walked up to the large glass wall and let my eyes wander across the city that was sprawled out in front of me like a picture. It was easily one of the most beautiful things that I'd ever seen. The hovering cars sped in the streets, and I couldn't help but think of how many extraordinarily strange people were just going about their days.

"Wait a minute. Time is frozen on the surface. Why aren't you?"

The sudden realization slapped me in the face like a brick wall.

"Time works differently here." The President waved me to the table and had me sit down. "Please take a seat. We need to do a few tests to legitimize your identity before we let you and your friends roam free in our city."

With that, a few more people entered the room in lab coats, carting big suitcases stuffed with machines.

I watched as they began to unload the various pieces of technology and set them up on the table in front of me.

I raised a brow at all of the technology that they'd dragged up just for me.

But if it made them less suspicious of me and gave the doctors more time to fix up Silas, I wasn't going to complain.

Plus, a huge part of me wanted to see what kind of tests they were going to do.

I drew the line at getting injected with things, but I was pretty open to other things.

As long as it got them off my back, it was fine with me.

The first person brought a small tablet and powered it before setting it in front of me, taking each of my fingers and pressing them against the screen and registering my fingerprints.

The next took a blood sample before moving across the table to process it, while another hooked up a cuff to my arm with a bunch of wires attached to it, the other end connected to a transparent computer. He swiped his finger across the screen a few times before turning to me.

"What is your name?"

"Eden Montgomery."

"Where are you from?"

"The water district."

"Do you mean us any harm?"

"Of course not. I didn't even know you existed until I was running for my life."

The President's eyes darted up to the doctor administering the test, and he nodded to her.

She glanced at the others whose tests had just finished, and they nodded to her too.

"No way." She smirked happily. "Bring them back in."

I didn't have the slightest clue what was happening, but the next thing I knew, the guys were being ushered back into the room, this time a lot less aggressively than before.

"What's going on?" Apollo asked.

"I don't know. They just realized that I have no reason to lie to them or something." I shrugged, more lost than ever.

"I apologize. I had to take every precaution. You know as well as I do what's at stake here, Madam founder."

I pulled my eyebrows together in confusion at what the hell she was talking about.

Maybe she'd finally just lost it. The stick in her ass must have slid up too far and caused massive bleeding and confusion.

"I have no idea what you're talking about." I said blankly.

One of the lab coat people leaned forward and whispered something in her ear, and she nodded.

"That makes sense."

"Actually, none of this is making any sense. I'd appreciate it if you could fill me in on whatever little charade you're trying to play? That would be great. " I smiled sarcastically.

"If you follow me, this will all make a lot more sense. Then a lot less sense. Followed by more sense." She got up from the table and, without another word, left the room.

The guys and I exchanged odd looks. Meanwhile, the people in lab coats were staring at me in amazement as all the other people had.

"Well, we better go follow her! What are you doing?" Adler waved me through.

I scrambled back into the hallway and met up with her halfway down the hall.

We walked in a thick, awkward silence until we made our way

back to the elevator.

It slowly started to descend, just like the feeling in the pit of my stomach until we made it to the ground floor, and I was sure we were going to stop. But instead, we kept going deeper until we reached the fifth floor under the bottom floor, and President Kim started down the dimly lit hallway.

These hallways weren't white and sterile. They were a deep and creepy shade of red.

And the lighting was soft and warm to match.

There were portraits of people hanging on the walls as we walked, and I noticed that they were all women, standing proudly.

"Who are these people?"

"These are all the people who built this city. The Presidents, ambassadors, and physicists who discovered groundbreaking things that became a backbone of our society." She paused in front of a random one that held a woman with long black hair. Her smile was wide, and her eyes were bright.

"She created the hovercraft technology." She moved further down the hall and stopped again. "She created the self-sustainable energy source that lights the entire city and copies the light of the sun and moon." She took another step. "And she created the self-healing nanotechnology that is fixing your friend's leg right now."

"All the amazing things. And I'm all for girl power, but I'm having a hard time figuring out what any of this means for me."

President Kim ignored my words and continued down the long hallway that curved to the left.

The second we rounded the curve, I noticed a portrait that hung at the very end, and I squinted at the familiarity.

There was no way what I was seeing was right. No way at all.

I had to rub at my eyes a few times.

I glanced back at the guys to make sure that they saw the same shit that I was, and they all nodded without me, even saying a single word.

We got to the portrait and stopped.

I noticed that in a glass case in front of it was the other time clock. It's particles glistening in black and white glittering particles. It reminded me of the stars floating around.

It was exactly what I was looking for.

Had this been the place the looking glass was leading me the entire time?

My eyes trailed back up to the portrait, standing large in its glory.

"And she founded the entire city over one hundred years ago."

I looked up to see a portrait of me, with my name etched in small golden letting beneath it.

Eden Montgomery. Founder.

Printed in Great Britain
by Amazon